TAKING

Forbidden Obsession Duet 2

LYNN BURKE

TAKING

Hot as a California summer and off limits.

Too young.

A rich, snobby princess, but I couldn't help crave her innocence as much as the next man.

No matter how much her feigned hatred stirred up obsessive want inside me, I found myself protecting her from the real predator.

Betrayed by Addilyn and my father, I ended up in jail for assault.

But I'm a free man now, and I have what I need to get my revenge.

I'll destroy the man who uprooted my life.

Make Addilyn pay for her part in ruining me.

My obsession has not waned in five years, so to hell with wanting.

This time, I'm taking.

Addilyn

Five Years Later...

My ears rang as I sat stiff as marble while Mother and Lloyd's lawyer read her will.

Mother had loved her alcohol, but she'd never once popped pills to escape reality. An overdose, the coroner had said, but I didn't believe the autopsy report. Refused to. Even after her funeral, I couldn't be swayed into thinking my mother would stoop to such a pedestrian level to take her own life.

She'd been living it up, having all that "me time" she'd bitched about wanting.

No more kids in the house.

No more responsibilities except for luncheons, parties, and spa treatments.

Even if she'd been miserable, she would have never taken her own life, merely out of fear of what her peers would say over her grave.

I felt sure Lloyd had something to do with her death, but I had no proof.

None.

She was gone. Mere ashes in a piece of pottery resting beneath the Alaskan soil.

She'd never truly wanted me, never loved me the way I'd needed with physical touch or kind words. I'd never been good enough, but I'd been unable to hate Mother—even when she constantly believed her husband's word over mine about how he'd sexually abused and tormented me for those two years.

The chair my stepfather had brought into his office for me pressed hard against my bony shoulder blades and tailbone through my pantsuit. I might have found strength in order to leave home, something I hadn't known I'd possessed through anger— but being in the presence of Lloyd swept my fortitude away like dead leaves in a winter's wind.

He made me weak rather than pissed off. Timid, regardless of my lifted chin and straight spine. Thickness tightened my throat to the point of pain.

A hot tear slid down my cheek, but it stemmed from disappointment in myself, not grief. I didn't bother to blot it with a tissue. It dripped free from my chin, splashing onto my clenched hands atop my lap.

I'd escaped their household, but he'd managed to gain control over me until I turned twenty-one.

I'm powerless again.

I swallowed against the harsh truth which ripped clear down to my stomach like jagged glass. I had moved out the day I graduated from high school, desperate for freedom from that monster. Gideon, Lloyd's son, had begged me to stay away from him. He'd been dragged away in cuffs for beating up my ex-friend, his only concern my safety. Mother had encouraged the decision for me to leave and seen to my expenses without question.

But she'd always been lavish with gifts, buying pretty much whatever I wanted. I'd figured that was how she'd shown the love she had for me. Or perhaps she had believed my accusations against her husband and thought caring for me monetarily would clear her of guilt for bringing that monster into our home. But with her gone and my inheritance in his hands…

Two months until I turned twenty-one, until I had access to the funds to keep up to date on the taxes for the house Mother had bought me, to pay college tuition, to pay bills, and to put food on the small table my only friend Ciarra and I shared. I just needed to stay out of Lloyd's hands until then.

"Do you have any questions, Miss Reed?" Mother's lawyer asked me, breaking through the blackness of my mind and making me aware of the nausea stirring at being in close proximity with my abuser.

Glancing over at Lloyd, I didn't bother answering the attorney. I'd heard enough—more than enough to chill and twist my insides up tight.

The heat in Lloyd's dark eyes said it all and only made me colder. I once more shivered under his stare as I'd often done beneath his bruising touch.

He was in charge, same as when Gideon sat behind bars and I had no one to protect me from Lloyd's advances. He would take what he wanted, or he would find a way to make me penniless, his steady gaze promised.

A tremor wracked through me, and I wrenched my focus off him before vomit rose to spew over his desk. Dark memories slithered upward, ones I'd shoved deep down into my bowels where I'd attempted to shit them out over the years. They stroked my mind with the same inky, putrid touch of Lloyd's fingertips. His cruel lips. The hard length that had stolen my innocence with so much pain I hadn't been able to find pleasure with anyone since, no matter how hard I tried—

"No. No questions. Excuse me," I choked out, hopping from my chair and rushing to the powder room as my stomach roiled.

Mere bile erupted from my gut, splattering into the toilet I hugged. My hands grasped the seat in a white-knuckled grip while I heaved over and over, as though my body tried to purge the memory of Lloyd from my life.

My face broke into a sweat from gagging so violently, and my hair stuck to my cheeks. Still, my insides rolled and clenched.

Never should have come.

Ciarra had begged me not to, but I'd had faith in my strength to look down my nose at him like the piece of shit he was. I'd expected closure from the reading of Mother's will. Hoped for it.

No such luck.

I'd have been better off showing up with a pitch-fork and stabbing him in the groin before making eye contact with the bastard who with one glance had me feeling like a powerless sixteen-year-old again.

Two months until I gained true freedom—

"Sweetheart." Lloyd's rumbling voice outside the bathroom door caused me to gag again, and I coughed, choking. "Are you alright?"

Eyes clenched shut, I rocked back onto my heels to suck oxygen into my lungs. "Fuck offf, Lloyd," I spat out and coughed again.

The doorknob turned, and dread rolled through me—I hadn't locked it.

Lloyd loomed over me in the small half-bath before I could stand, putting his groin right in front of my face.

I turned my head away from him, my stomach flayed open as memories crashed into my head, shrouding my mind with darkness and making every cell in my body as weak as a baby seal.

"Sweetheart, look at me."

My stomach heaved again at the same words that haunted my nightmares, but nothing came up. Forced to my knees. Jaw pried open. Gagging and tears over the pain in my throat and his whispers of me being a good girl.

Eventually, I had stopped fighting. What was the point? I'd been without a choice, a toy for him to fuck with—

"Addilyn Jane."

A sob ripped from my lips as Lloyd grasped me beneath the arm pits and hauled me up against his hard chest. Panic lay dormant from years of repetitive trauma.

"No! P-Please, don't!" I couldn't find the strength to do more than whisper and wish for a knife to stab into his balls.

"Shh." He caressed my back, his lips against the top of my head as I struggled to push his heavier weight away. "There's nothing you can do about this," he murmured, his arms a vise around me. "I knew from the first time Ingrid showed me a picture of her beautiful daughter that you were always meant to be mine. I've gone three years without you… and now that she's dead, we can finally be together."

"I was meant to be Gideon's!" I cried out what I knew would piss him off.

"And he hates you for what you did to him," Lloyd reminded me.

The monster had informed me of that fact after his son got sentenced for assault on the first boy to kiss me.

"He doesn't want to see you ever again."

I went limp in his arms and sobbed against the memory of the heartbreak I'd felt in that moment in the courthouse. The pain and emptiness I relived every time I remembered what I had done, responsible for Gideon's incarceration.

I shouldn't have told the truth under oath.

Doing so would have saved him jail time—and my innocence.

"I can soothe your torment, sweetheart," Lloyd murmured against my hair. "Let me."

Soothe my torment…he'd never done anything but provoke it. Self-loathing for my body's involuntary arousal to the pain he'd caused helped me summon the strength to fight.

"No!" Eyes shut tight, I wrenched my head away from his searching lips, his lips ghosting over my ear.

"Don't fight me," he said, all trace of nicety gone from his voice as his grip tightened around my arms, clenching me hard enough to bruise. "I hold your life in my hands, Addilyn. Every penny you stand to inherit is mine unless you do exactly as I say."

"I'm not some teenage kid you can threaten anymore, Lloyd," I choked out through the tears rolling down my cheeks, still straining to keep my mouth from his searching one. Heat flushed through my body, tensing my muscles. "I won't be owned. I won't be manipulated. Let *go* of me!"

"There will be rules."

Fuck that. I'd had enough of his rules.

I'm strong. Resilient.

Lies, but I needed them in order to survive.

My attempt to stomp on his foot with my heel scuttled us sideways into the bathroom wall, knocking a painting to the tile floor. "No!"

The pressure from his hands holding me intensified to the point I cried out from the pain. "First, you're going to grow your hair back out so I have something to grip while making love to you."

"Let me *go*!"

"And you're going to start wearing all that sparkly makeup like when you were fifteen so you look young again."

I screamed my rage at the memories crashing into my mind and attempted to bite his arm. He wrenched me around, holding my back against his hard chest, his face pressed to my neck so I couldn't headbutt him. My chest ached as my lungs fought to draw breath.

"You'll obey my rules—or I'll leave you with nothing," he hissed, his breath hot on my ear. "No house. No money. No place to call your home. You'll be penniless without me."

"D-Don't care." I yanked my arms hard enough that his fingertips marked my skin, his threats no longer heavy enough to make me care about the outcome. "Let me go!"

"Never," he growled—and bit my damn lobe.

"Stop!" I shrieked at the zing rushing to my core that caused me to tremble with shame. I twisted and attempted to turn to escape what I didn't want, but his hold proved relentless.

Those fantasies I'd had as a teenager about being tied up? Taken by force?

Lloyd had obliterated them to the pits of hell even though his bruising touch had roused my body to life every damn time.

I feared the dark. Feared the thought of blind-folds, of ropes, of being restrained in any way—

"You're going to dress like a slut again, not this matronly pants and blouse shit. I want you teasing me with your short skirts and tight shirts showing off these gorgeous tits..." He licked the shell of my ear and squeezed my breast hard enough I gasped—against the pain and the beginnings of arousal I hadn't felt in years.

Sick—I'm so damn sick.

"Obey me, and I'll give you the world."

Lloyd had attempted to "give me the world" once before, and all I'd ended up with was bouts of depression that lasted for months on end and night-mares that continued to haunt me three years after escaping him. The type of PTSD flare ups that hindered my ability to trust others and make friends.

"Give in, Addilyn. You'll never be free of me."

I knew from past experience the only option I had was to relax and let him have his way. The first, I could do. I'd promised myself the second wouldn't ever happen again.

One day...*some*day, I would make him pay for stealing my innocence.

Letting out a heavy exhale, I forced my instincts I'd grown back in my time away from him to quiet so I could go limp in his arms. I allowed Lloyd to hold me like he was my everything—what the sick fuck had always lusted after and never accomplished no matter how hard he'd tried.

I had claimed no man would break me again like he'd done. And while I had escaped him physically, the sickness he'd intensified in me remained—but I refused to bend to my weakness.

"There's my sweetheart," he murmured, gently turning me to face him once more.

Dark eyes, full of want peered down at me as he smiled.

My stomach heaved, but I swallowed the bile down, chin lifting.

I am strong.

My lips rose—and I jerked my knee upward with every bit of strength I possessed.

"Ah!" Lloyd let out harsh grunt and jerked backward into the hallway, hands dropping to cup his nuts I'd attempted to cave in. Too bad I didn't have a knife to slice them off. Bent over like he was, I didn't hesitate.

I used my knee again but smashed it up into his face. He topped over backward, blood spurting from his nose. Satisfaction coursed through me at his groan.

"Sick fuck!" I spat on his face and sprinted on shaky legs to the office for my purse, my pulse pounding with adrenaline, my breaths rasped. My breast still tingled with a pain/pleasure that caused my stomach to roil again.

The lawyer had left, so I grabbed my belongings and hurried back into the hallway, hovering on the verge of losing my shit. My slip-ons slapped the marble beneath them.

Lloyd still lay groaning where I'd left him outside the powder room moaning like a pussy, and I rushed past, his grunted, "You'll be sorry!" propelling me forward. Sobs let loose to echo around the ostentatious chandelier in the vast foyer where I'd first met him and my protector who'd failed me.

The one *I* had failed.

Gideon.

I slammed the heavy oak door behind me, wishing to return to that brief moment five years earlier when Gideon had covered my back with warmth and hardness there on the porch. He had caused my skin to shiver in the best way possible even though I had hated my body's unwanted response to his nearness at the time.

He'd been the only man I hadn't shied away from when cornered...

His father had ravaged me while I lived unwillingly in his house, under his sweaty body and heavy hand.

He took my innocence. Ruined my mind and body. And now he can take everything else.

Everything legally owed to me, my inheritance. The roof over my head, the food from my table. But I would rot in hell before I bent over for his dick like I'd been forced to do for two years. All the while, Mother had accused me of being a jealous, lying bitch.

I hadn't spoken to her in three years—and I wouldn't miss her one goddamn bit.

She'd brought a snake into our home, and I would gladly go homeless in the Alaskan wilderness before making myself vulnerable to his abuse ever again.

$$2$$

Gideon

Jail sucked ass, and not in the good way with a little tongue action.

No pussy.

Disgusting food.

No fucking freedom.

It'd been stolen from me all for bloodying some asshole's nose. The sheriff's son, the one who I'd caught taking my stepsister's first kiss. I'd enjoyed the feel of his nose crunching beneath my fist, his blood splattering across my sweatshirt. He was lucky I hadn't completely lost my shit on his ass—or I'd have gotten locked up for murder rather than assault.

The second I'd gotten hauled off in cuffs, it seemed like I had ceased to exist for those on the outside. Not even Dad had visited or called. Good thing too, since I didn't have to deal with attempted manipulation, empty excuses, or the sight of the princess bitch who haunted my memory even after five years behind bars.

For the first couple of months, I'd fought off the beginnings of depression on a daily basis. My mind wanted to wallow in the fucking shit of despair rather than focus on the revenge I'd promised myself while sitting in the courtroom—and I'd flagged in my determination to keep my head above water.

They'd thought I'd had anger issues as a juvenile. Fucking nothing compared to the influence of the mundane and having true criminals in close proximity.

Rage became my best friend, one I coddled deep in my soul and fed with thoughts of getting back at those who'd betrayed me. I expended my aggression and excess anger on the assholes locked up with me who needed a beating.

Halfway through year two, I got a new cell mate —fucking funny-assed twink who offered the use of his body to ease my daily morning wood, but I refused. My fist would do until my release.

His constant smile and his glass-half full attitude became my lifeline to sanity, to not losing my shit and giving in to the darkness that hovered in my periphery.

I learned to control my rage because of him. Keep it under lock and key. I took fucking pride in hiding the truth of the kind of man I was deep inside my fucked up head—same as him.

Twinkie sat in the slammer alongside me for stabbing his bastard of a father in the chest over a dozen times after years of mental and emotional abuse. How the fuck he continued to smile...I'd decided he was missing some marbles upstairs, but the guy was still smart as fuck.

He was in for life with no family but a shit ton of contacts on the outside. A hundred acre lot closer to Fairbanks was the only physical thing he had left to his name, thanks to a great uncle he'd never met.

He'd planned to live off the grid up there after the intentional murder, back down one hell of a two-mile dirt driveway in a cabin he hadn't seen in since childhood—and wouldn't ever lay eyes on again according to his sentence.

Twinkie and I had dreamed of escaping jail. Living out in the sticks. Studied how it was done, from snaring animals to tanning hides.

My depression gave way to determination, the kind that propelled a man forward to stick to his desires, regardless of obstacles.

Twinkie gave me back my reason to live, helping me plan my revenge for the day I stepped outside the prison. My list accounted for four individuals: Sheriff Bradshaw and his son Devon, Addilyn Reed, and my father, Lloyd Destil.

And I would have my revenge, come hell or high

water. The sheriff would end up in jail, his son would be ruined, the princess would break beneath my mind and body, and the last? He might have been the sperm donor who gave me life, but I would end his.

During years three through five without freedom, I focused on my health too. My strength, both physically and mentally. I gained thirty or so pounds of pure muscle—and used what I'd built to protect Twinkie and the other guys who couldn't stand up for themselves against the raping bastards inside with us who'd gone too long without a woman.

I'd lost my goddamn mind the first time one of the other inmates touched me, a couple of days after getting locked up. Guess they thought I'd be easy pickings. Knocked his ass out cold—and no one tried to grab mine after that.

I ended up in solitary for that fight, but I'd drawn a line, letting the other fuckers rotting away with me know that I wouldn't be fucked with—and I turned my focus on playing the game. I behaved and kept to myself except for those dark corners where no cameras existed and I could beat the shit out of or shank anyone who deserved it. I kicked asses in secret and kissed others, hoping my lies would earn me an early parole after only serving a partial sentence.

A supposed poster boy convict—and I fucking walked.

Guess that fucking Sheriff Bradshaw who had seemed above the law didn't have any sway beyond getting me tossed into jail.

And I'd heard and learned enough from Twinkie and his boyfriend, seen enough in those five years to know how to hit him—hard. Make it hurt.

"You're going to write to me every week," Twinkie said, squeezing me tight.

I allowed him to rub his baby-like face against my chest, to enjoy the feel of my hard body he'd often begged for.

"Promise," I told him, slapping his back in a real bro hug rather than the lover's embrace he would have preferred. "And find someone better than Rogers, you hear me?"

Twinkie stepped back and winked, his smirk making me roll my eyes.

"Can't believe you actually like that fucker. He's ugly as shit and doesn't treat you much better."

"He's got a gorgeous dick," my cellmate said with a shrug. His smile faded as footsteps approached our cell. "You take that information he gave you and make them pay, G."

Information—evidence—to link the sheriff to the reason Rogers sat in jail. And the best part? The fucker didn't even know it existed.

Above the law, my ass. Within a matter of weeks, he'd be in cuffs. Behind bars.

And if shit kept me from going through with my

plan? I'd find a dark alley and end his life like I did the two men whose demise earned me Roger's trust.

I gave Twinkie a tight nod—and the guard showed up at our door.

"Take care," Twinkie whispered, his hazel eyes welling with tears.

I wished I'd been able to love him, to offer him the attention beyond the occasional snuggle he was always desperate for when waking from nightmares.

"Sorry I couldn't be more for you, Twinkie."

"You were everything I needed at this time in my life." His flashing smile spoke of forced happiness. "I'll find myself another hunk of man flesh to hold me after my bad dreams. Maybe the next one will let me suck on his nuts in exchange."

I held his stare, clasping his hand hard until our cell door slid open.

No more words passed between us, and as the door slammed shut once more behind me, a real future ahead, I hoped he *would* find a man to love him like he wanted.

My only friend in the world, one I definitely could trust to not betray me like the other had done five years earlier.

I stepped beyond the correctional facilities' main doors, the winter coat I'd been given hitched up around my damn ears.

Fucking January in Alaska. Dark as shit. Cold as fuck, even though I had the burning need for revenge to keep me warm. But I had no one to meet me like in the movies when an innocent soul finds their freedom.

Chin tucked to my hollow-feeling chest, I headed down the stairs and toward the parking lot.

Even though Dad hadn't visited me, he'd wired me the state allowed five-hundred bucks every month. All five years. Hating him still came easily though. Forgiveness for uncovering my juvie records to send me to jail couldn't be bought. Determined to never touch the money, I'd held out until Twinkie had arrived.

His love of Jolly Ranchers and his occasional tears had me dipping into Dad's money. Eventually, I bought a pack of the Swedish Fish I'd always stared at while visiting the commissary on Twinkie's behalf.

Addilyn's favorite.

They tasted like I imagined her mouth did. Sweet. Cherries.

Probably fucking delicious.

I'd never had her mouth on any part of my body except wrapped around my dick that one time, the night before my arrest. The supposed non-consensual blowjob when I'd been riding high on a blood rage, desperate for release since I hadn't found it in beating Devon Bradshaw's face to shit and putting him in a two-day coma.

She'd spilled to her best friend Jenny what we'd done, and Jenny told the sheriff who had the prosecuting attorney bring it up while Addilyn sat on the stand.

The innocent princess had been embarrassed as hell and wouldn't look at me.

My dick chubbed up inside my jeans regardless of the howling wind spitting snowflakes at my face and the constant anger simmering deep in my gut that I'd become practiced at hiding.

The memory of Addilyn gave me daily boners, but her betrayal required restitution, same as how Dad would pay for his part in putting me away. Fuck his gifted money.

In boots a size too small, I trudged southward, toward Anchorage. I needed to find a place to crash for a few days. I'd use Dad's money to get myself a car and set the plan I'd been working on into motion —paid for by his own goddamn hand.

Talk about poetic fucking justice.

A dark SUV slowed alongside me not fifty yards from the penitentiary.

I moved off onto the berm, but the passenger window rolled down. I pulled up short.

Dark eyes lined with more wrinkles than had

been around them five years earlier peered across the console, meeting my gaze.

The need for violence burst open like a geyser I struggled to keep a cap on. "The fuck you want?" I asked Lloyd, my voice tight and my hands fisting at my sides.

"I came to pick up my son."

"I don't need to be picked up." Jaw clenched, I started forward once more, my bowels twisting over him showing up and ruining the surprise I'd had planned. The sheriff must have told him I'd gotten out early.

Wheels crunched on stone as he kept pace beside me. "Get in the car, Gideon."

"Fuck off, *Lloyd*," I spat back, my pulse pounding.

"It's January, you aren't wearing a hat, and it's ten fucking degrees. Get in the goddamn car."

Seeing as how the tips of my ears and nose had grown numb, I decided to put up with his presence for a few minutes.

Couldn't hurt, right? Not me, anyway.

I climbed into the SUV, the blast of heat doing little to thaw the chill that had reigned in my chest since my arrest five years earlier.

"I have a job for you," Dad said as though a day hadn't passed since we'd last spoken.

"Don't need a fucking job," I grunted, edginess twitching my muscles.

"Last time I checked," he said, pulling onto the

highway, "you just got out of jail, and you still owe me one."

I huffed a laugh. "Those juvie records of mine you supposedly did away with got uncovered. I don't owe you jack shit."

"I had nothing to do with that," he stated, his tone level. "But the monthly cash *was* from my pocket."

"And why the fuck should I believe you?"

"Because Sheriff Bradshaw has connections I don't. He's the one who found out about your stints in juvie—it wasn't from me."

I didn't believe a word he said, so I kept silent while studying his profile. Furrowed brow, strong nose—both inherited by me, both of which I wanted to ruin with my fists. The side view of him wasn't as easy to read as a full-on face, but I still felt sure he lied.

"Did you hear about Ingrid?" he asked, not looking at me.

His selfish cunt of a wife who'd rubbed off on her daughter more than I had expected.

"Overdose," I muttered what I'd heard through the grapevine. "But I'm thinking she got under your skin, and you finally decided to do away with her like you did your last wife to take advantage of being a grieving widow."

"She had a separate will that left everything to Addilyn."

Everything...

Well, fuck. I bit back a laugh, figuring out exactly where our conversation headed. He thought I was some badass motherfucker, a hopeless criminal for life since I'd spent time behind bars. "I hope you put money of your own aside," I said, unable to keep the snark and satisfaction from of my voice.

"I have control over the estate until—"

"The princess turns twenty-one," I tossed out what I suspected.

"Exactly."

"And I suppose you want me to take care of that little problem?"

His lips twitched as he kept watch on the road—and tapped the side of his nose to let me know I'd guessed right.

Heat flushed through my body. I had made plans for Addilyn already, and while most of what I'd fantasized about involved her pussy and a hate fuck with my dick that hadn't gotten action outside my hand in years, I had every intention of drawing blood too. Ruining her both physically and financially for what she'd done to me.

But the mental aspect of playing with her head would come first. She deserved to be fucked up emotionally like I'd been. I'd already thought along the lines Lloyd suggested.

"She's the one who got you put behind bars," Lloyd continued when I didn't give him the answer he wanted.

Like I needed reminding. I'd heard her one-worded answer that had slammed the final nail in my coffin.

Yes.

Hated that fucking word.

"It was her testimony that sealed your fate, Gideon. She should pay for what she did, and taking everything away from her, leaving the spoiled brat destitute, would be beautiful, wouldn't you agree?"

Of course he would know I agreed.

I eyed him while he drove, wet, heavy flakes of snow slapping at the windshield. Did he think I'd stayed a stupid seventeen-year-old during my stint in jail? "I'm not a dumb fuck, Lloyd. You've got no damn foot to stand on with Addilyn Reed still breathing unless you can get her to fall for you like you did Ingrid."

A muscle ticked in his smooth-shaven jaw, letting me know he'd failed. Even though the princess deserved what she had coming, a sense of… satisfaction over her escaping him swelled inside me.

"She needs to disappear," Lloyd said. "For good."

"And what makes you think I'd be willing to take care of your little problem?"

"Have the anger management classes helped?" he asked rather than answering—and he had a fucking point I didn't mind admitting to him.

"No."

"Then I expect when faced with the chance for revenge on that bitch, you'll want to take it."

I'd rather take her ass, make her cry, and laugh in her goddamn face as she broke beneath me.

"After your sentencing, I asked her why she did it," Lloyd said, turning into a hotel's parking lot.

I waited, giving him time to pull up in front of the main entrance, my head consumed with the memories of that day in court. My hands fisted, rage twisting my insides up tight.

"She called you a lying jackass, a twisted pervert who deserved to rot in jail. She claimed you sexually abused her countless times and that if you hadn't gotten put away for hurting her precious Devon, she would have told Ingrid everything you'd done to her —and charged you with statutory rape."

That little whore...

My teeth clenched as I sucked oxygen through my nose while remembering how she'd strode out of the courtroom, her haughty chin lifted. "She lied. I never fucking touched her," I all but spat, the anger on constant simmer in my gut hazing my vision. So much for my fucking self-control.

That spoiled princess got to me every goddamn time. Clouded my mind. Pissed me off.

"She gave her innocence to Devon that same night in our den while you lay on a hard cot facing ten long years in prison."

I bit back a snarl at Lloyd's words. *Fucking cunt*

whore... "Thought you wanted that bit of flesh for yourself."

Lloyd turned to face me fully, coolness in his eyes. "It was never about Addilyn—I truly adored Ingrid."

"Liar," I called him out, knowing I spoke the truth.

He narrowed his gaze but didn't turn away. "Yes, I loved Addilyn—but as a daughter, not sexually. She reminded me of a young Ingrid, the only woman for me. How could I not notice her beauty? Her budding sexuality? That doesn't mean I wanted to fuck my stepdaughter, Gideon."

He spewed shit from between his lips, rehearsed lines in attempts to cover his greed, but none of that mattered any longer.

I had my plan, and while Lloyd showing up definitely switched things around for me as far as who would pay first, I could still accomplish what I'd been dreaming about for the past five years, what Twinkie and his boyfriend, Rogers, had helped me put together.

"Where is she?"

"Ingrid bought her a house not far from the university." Lloyd handed me a folded piece of paper, making the task of finding her easier. "Take her, have your revenge, and call me when you're done."

"Done as in six feet under," I asked, "or leave her a bloody mess of flesh for you to finish off?"

He grimaced but smoothed out his face in an attempt to appear unaffected by the violence that lay in the deepest part of my being. "I wish to have a final word with her, so I would prefer her in one piece."

I dipped my head, shoving the paper into my coat pocket.

"Hotel." Lloyd motioned toward the entrance with his chin. "Your room has been paid for through the end of the week. I have the same cell number, so call me once you've completed your job."

Oh, I'd be calling him, alright. But it wouldn't be with the news he expected.

———————————

3

Addilyn

———————————

"Leo has been asking about you."

I glanced up from my toast, eyeing my only friend and roommate as she poured a cup of coffee. She turned and winked at me.

I rolled my eyes, annoyed I had to remind her of my truth. Again. "I'm all done with men."

"He's a sweetheart," Ciarra told me, a phrase she'd tossed out countless times.

The kind of man who wouldn't rouse my hormones no matter how hard he tried, no matter how good a kisser or gentle a lover he might be.

"Therapy hasn't helped, so what makes you believe fucking another good guy will?" I asked and forced myself to take another bite of my bland breakfast.

She let out a sigh and wrapped her fleece robe tighter around her chest before sitting down across from me. "I think once you find the right person, things will be better for you."

My throat tightened, and I studied my toast for the next bite I didn't want to take but would anyway. I'd lost enough weight in the past couple of years. Any more, and the winter winds would blow me off my feet.

Ciarra knew about my past. Lloyd. The abuse. Mother and her jealousy.

She was also aware of the fact that I didn't enjoy sex, that only the sharpest of pain inflicted by Lloyd had ever roused that part of me after Gideon's arrest. Or perhaps it was Gideon's touch that had ruined me first.

Either way, life had been so easy before Gideon's arrest. Nothing to truly worry over…

"It's time to move on." Ciarra grasped my wrist and squeezed lightly, keeping me grounded in the present rather than wilting beneath my past's dark memories.

I knew she spoke the truth, but the idea of trying again chilled me through. "I'm broken beyond repair."

"You're not," she snipped, straightening in her chair. "You're beautiful. Caring. Empathetic and worthy of a good man's love. Hell," she said, snorting a huffed laugh, "you deserve it for all the shit fate has dished out on you."

My lips tilted upward as I remembered slamming my knee into Lloyd's nose. "I do, don't I?"

"Karma ought to be on her knees begging your forgiveness." Her green eyes blazed, and I found my smile widening, warmth growing inside me "You're so damn stubborn—you're always telling yourself that you're broken when in reality, you won't allow yourself the chance to evolve. Or even *try* to change for that matter."

"I went to therapy, and I dated two guys."

"Two guys. Two dicks. You need to experience a hell of a lot more than that to *move on* sexually."

"Says the woman who's been dating the same guy she lost her virginity to last year."

Ciarra's cheeks flushed. "When you find the one who twitterpates your heart, you know."

"Twitterpates." I snorted. Ciarra and her love of older animated movies cracked me up. "You're the only person I trust, you know," I told her, my smile fading as another ex-friend who had enjoyed movies came to mind, weighing me down. The one who had betrayed me.

"And I wish I had a second brother to cherish you so I could call you my sister for real."

Forcing away thoughts of Jenny, I considered Ciarra's words. Her one older brother, Roan, had found his love in the wilds of Alaska—and they lived off grid with their two kids closer to Fairbanks.

Ciarra had grown up on an even more primitive homestead but had sought a different life once she had turned eighteen, got her GED, and decided on college.

We met when I'd been fresh out of Lloyd and Mother's home. I'd been hesitant to trust, but like with the wild critters from her homestead, she wooed me in. Once she broke through my aversion to be vulnerable again, I clung to her with all my might—and she continued to allow it even when I lost myself to moments of remembered horror.

The Addilyn Whisperer, I called her, my Ciarra Kelly.

"You *are* my sister," I told her, my throat tightening up.

"And because you love me," she said with a wink, "you're going to trust me on this. Go out with Leo. Let him buy you dinner. It can be a simple baby step —he won't push for more. He's not that type."

"You're sure?" I had no room in my life for anyone remotely like Lloyd—even if no one had managed to arouse my body since.

"I'm sure," she stated with a smile, without a doubt knowing exactly what I thought. "Give it a shot, Addilyn."

Baby steps…simple dinner.

I could do small talk if there was no expectation of connecting or fucking.

Letting out a heavy exhale, I nodded. "Okay."

"Yes!" Ciarra squealed. "He's such a sweetie! You're going to love him. Everything will work out, Addilyn. I promise."

I'd been promised so many damn things over the years...and the only one to keep his word had been ripped away from me. Hated me.

My throat clogged again, and I stood, taking the remains of my breakfast to the trash barrel.

We trudged through two inches of fresh snow on the uncleared sidewalks toward class, bundled up against the winter weather. I breathed deeply, the sting of cold up through my nostrils and filling my lungs making me feel alive, something I struggled with on a daily basis.

"It's been two weeks," Ciarra said from beside me. "Do you think he's decided to let you go?"

My lips thinned at the reminder of Lloyd and what had transpired over the reading of Mother's will. I'd come home and told Ciarra—and she held me as I sobbed until I passed out.

A shiver slid down my spine, one that caused me to straighten. I whipped my head around.

"What?" Ciarra asked as I studied the sidewalk and the few people hurrying through the biting wind.

That feeling…that energy I remembered all too well…

Shaking my head, I turned forward. Faced reality. Gideon sat in jail for at least five more years.

"Do you think Lloyd is stalking you?" Ciarra whispered, stepping closer to my side.

"No," I didn't hesitate in replying. Lloyd's presence hadn't ever given me the kind of shiver Gideon's had whenever we shared space.

"Maybe he has someone trailing you—waiting to grab you when you least expect it."

Something Lloyd could probably get away with, considering he and the sheriff were thick as thieves.

Ciarra linked her arm through mine, even though out thick coats made us waddle around like padded penguins. "Until your birthday, it might be best to not be alone, if you know what I mean."

Growing up as she had, Ciarra tended toward nervousness and being extra careful when it came to "bad guys." As for me, I sometimes wondered what the point was. I'd already been ruined.

"I'm sure it's nothing," I muttered, hitching my chin into my scarf. "I'm never by myself in public, and I never go out. What's he going to do? Break into our house and steal me away in the middle of the night?"

"Still. He said you'd be sorry for not giving him what he wanted. Is there any legal action he might try?"

"Not that I'm aware of." But I didn't know. Perhaps I needed to make a call to Mother's old lawyer and dig a little deeper into what I faced over the next two months. The reminder twisted my stomach up.

Ciarra squeezed my arm tighter, and minutes later we breathed in relief as warmth from the science building swarmed over us. It still took me twenty minutes into the professor's lecture before I shrugged out of my coat. With hardly any fat on my body, I was always cold.

Shivering.

Pasty-pale as hell.

I no longer bothered with the makeup I'd been enamored with as a teenager to cover up the pallor of my skin. Intentionally, I wore baggy clothing to hide my bone rack body and the breasts that refused to shrink. Frumpy clothes, the bobbed hair I'd always wanted, and an unpainted face made me background noise in crowds—exactly as I wished to be.

The bubbly rich girl who befriended everyone had morphed into an inhibited, quiet wallflower.

Unnoticed.

Safe from the attentions of men.

But when Ciarra and I once more stepped into the cold, heading to our next class, that tingling awareness raised the hair on my arms.

A scan around the immediate area didn't reveal anyone lingering, no dark-tinted, windowed cars.

Lack of sleep.

I let out a heavy, annoyed exhale at myself.

Still, I held onto my friend's arm like a lifeline.

4

Gideon

Addilyn had cut her hair.

The ends stuck out beneath her knit hat a few inches above her shoulders, haphazard and without the sleek look she'd had as a teenager.

She didn't wear makeup.

And the coat covering her from neck to knees? It appeared second hand, definitely not name brand like the rich snob used to go for.

A dark-haired girl clung to her side, and they huddled together while going from class to class throughout the day.

I sat in a clunker Subaru I'd gotten for a few grand, the heater at least in top notch shape. Fucker kept me warm and toasty while I watched my prey.

The two women stopped at a grocery store after classes, and I braved the cold to get a better look. I needed a few staples anyway. With my own hat and scarf I'd picked up from the discount store the day after my release, I'd be hidden enough that she wouldn't recognize me.

She let her coat gap open after perusing three aisles, and I allowed myself a good stare across the short distance separating us.

Pale face. Flatlined lips. Baggy shirt...generic brand jeans a size or three too large. Addilyn no longer held her chin up like a prissy bitch, but her neck still made my fingertips itch to squeeze and my teeth to graze and bite. Damn attraction flared even after all I'd been through—and I fucking hated it.

Shoulders hunched beneath the weight of her winter coat, Addilyn ambled beside her friend, their quiet voices occasionally reaching me as I followed along at a distance with my own basket in hand.

She'd changed drastically in five years.

Due to Lloyd's handling? I doubted it had been her mother's death that caused the shroud of depression that seemed to hang over her head. They'd never gotten along, and if I had to bet, Addilyn probably hadn't shed a single tear over Ingrid's grave.

I crept closer, needing to see her eyes, to read the emotions she'd always worn on her face like an open book.

Too close.

Her spine straightened, and she jerked around as

though feeling the energy that had always seemed to tether us together.

I dropped into a crouch, faced the shelves of canned goods, and lifted my shoulder enough so most of my profile would be hidden.

Green beans, low sodium, I noted on the can in my hand.

Fucking gross, but I dropped it in the basket on my other side, keeping my face turned away.

"Addilyn?" her friend called.

"Yeah. Sorry." She let out a small, shuddered exhale, and I dared another peek her way.

She followed after the dark-haired girl—Ciarra Kelly. Roommate. Best and only friend if her lack of a social life over the ten days I'd been following her indicated the truth.

Addilyn didn't do spontaneous. She didn't step out of her daily routine.

Breakfast at the small table in their kitchen beside a bay window.

Off to classes at seven forty-five.

Lunch in the cafeteria.

Straight home at the end of the day—except for groceries twice in those ten days.

Knowing her home life proved just as easy since she lived in a single-floor home with plenty of windows.

A few nights, Ciarra went out or her boyfriend came over, but Addilyn never deviated from her usual small dinner she picked at, TV, movies, or reading with a cup of herbal tea sans sweetener, and bed.

Lamb to the slaughter for an observant fucker like me.

But I held off, enjoying the fuck out of the adrenaline high of stalking. Watching. Riding the edge of excitement to finally have her in my grasp. Soon she'd be beneath me where she belonged, taking the pain I planned on dishing out like an all you can eat buffet.

I'd gotten my fill of real, good food but had yet to taste pussy.

Almost six years I'd gone without since being uprooted from California—and the only warm, wet hole I wanted belonged to Addilyn Jane Reed.

My betrayer.

My obsession.

She and Ciarra paid and left, and I flashed my dimples at the cashier, offering a wink that didn't promise jack shit. Flushed cheeks on a female—thin, thick, gorgeous, or plain, I soaked that shit in.

There was so much damn beauty around. Men holding out for perfection didn't realize the opportunities they missed.

I didn't have to wait either—but Addilyn was what I wanted. What I would take when the time was right.

My princess used to be a smart girl. Intuitive and alert.

She and Ciarra left a spare key beneath their welcome mat on the stoop.

Seriously.

And letting myself into their private space at two in the morning was a piece of cake. No dog, no fucking alarm. Closest neighbors were far enough away that they wouldn't see a goddamn thing in the dark night.

I walked in like I owned the place—not that I complained about my luck.

After I slipped off my shoes just inside the front door, I let my socked feet feather touch the floor before putting my full weight down. One squeaky oak board beneath had me jerking my foot back, and I tried again, finding a quieter area to step.

Across the living room, a nightlight in the hallway beyond made trekking across the small space a breeze.

Three doors—bathroom wide open and the other two were bedrooms, I expected.

I eyed the one farther down the hallway while adrenaline coursed through my veins. It was set back, away from the entrance, from the space where people might congregate. Not that the two women had company outside of Ciarra's boyfriend.

Addilyn had changed enough that I knew she would try to hide like she did with the baggy clothes that covered a body I remembered all too well.

I bypassed the closest bedroom, and my heart rate jacked. Shoulders hitched with tension, ready to snap if found out.

The house's heating system kicked on with a tired groan, and I paused my slow stride for a second.

Nothing human stirred, so I moved forward at a faster clip, the sound of the return sucking air enough to smother whatever noise I might make.

I grasped the door handle, slowly inhaled through my nose, and twisted it quietly until I allowed myself a few inches to peer through.

A nightlight lit Addilyn's face from where she huddled along the twin bed's edge. White-blonde hair lay a rumpled mess on her pillow, much shorter than I'd remembered but no less beautiful. A comforter tucked beneath her chin that hugged to her chest rather than lifted in the air with her usual snobbery.

Dark lashes fluttered against pale cheeks, and above were dark slashes of eyebrows perfectly shaped and natural in color even though the hue of her hair indicated otherwise.

A contradiction, the mystery of which I couldn't wait to unravel.

A gorgeous, dick-thickening piece of ass I planned on taking in more ways than one.

But not tonight.

I stared at her through the barely opened door, memories rushing through my mind of our shared Jack and Jill bathroom. My horny ass catching a peek of her whenever I could.

Her watching me jack off in my bed.

Her stealing a look at me in the shower.

Her lush mouth wrapped around my dick.

Fuck.

I grabbed the bulge growing in my jeans, teeth clenched and lips parted while she slept peacefully. No worries, no cares other than spending Mother's cash on getting her degree in marine biology—wherever the fuck that passion had come from.

I'd expected her to go into business, perhaps marketing for all the trendy makeup shit she'd been into back in high school.

The Addilyn I'd known prior to jail certainly wasn't the same young woman lying in the bed feet away from me.

She rolled to her back, letting out an exhale, and I stepped into the shadows, closing the door to a mere crack. A shiver wracked through her body, and she let out a whimper that sounded like fear rather than a sensual one.

Brow furrowing, I studied her twitches. Wondered over the quiet noises she made—

A quiet gasp and her entire body jerked before quickly stilling, her breaths heavy. "Damnit," she muttered, rubbing her face.

I eased the door shut, gently returned the handle in place so it wouldn't click, and hurried up the hallway in my socked feet, curiosity over what she'd dreamed of filling my head. Fear? And if so, from what? Did she know I followed her? Did she know Lloyd wanted her gone?

Whatever she'd dreamed about, it had woken her up enough that I had to get the hell out of the house.

Her bedroom door squeaked, and I detoured from the front door to the couch and shifted to a silent crouch behind its threadbare bulk. I dropped to a plank and eased my body down flat, breath held.

My heart raced, and I grinned, riding the high of fucking life. Freedom.

Footsteps shuffled toward the kitchen, and I inched my body forward along the floor to peek around the couch's edge, fighting to keep my breaths shallow so she wouldn't hear.

My fucking shoes sat inside the door on their entry rug.

With my body tensed to hop up if needed, I watched Addilyn in a long T-shirt fill a glass with water from the tap. Pale legs—thinner than I remembered. Bony ankles and knees.

Brow furrowing, I lifted my gaze up over the bump of her ass to shoulder blades that had no business protruding from the thin shirt covering her stooped form.

Her head tipped back as she drank her water down. Once finished, she set it in the sink.

A shudder rippled over her, and I pulled back, knowing she would turn, that she could sense the same energy I did whenever I got too close to her.

My insides jittered, and I closed my eyes, wanting to laugh like a goddamn fool from the adrenaline rushing through my blood.

She feels me...same as I do her.

The hairs on my arms rose like an electrical current raced over my skin as I waited. Ears strained beyond the pulse thumping between them. Body tensed—to fight or flee depending on the outcome of my breaking and entering.

Addilyn let out a heavy exhale, and her shuffling footsteps disappeared back down the hallway.

The bedroom door snicked shut.

I let out a breath I hadn't realized I'd held.

After a quick push up to a plank, I stood to find myself alone as expected.

Unsure if I was happy over that fact, I whispered my feet over the floor, put back on my shoes, and let myself out into the cold.

My fingers itched to take, but the waiting, the prolonged wanting would only make my revenge that much sweeter. If the state of her thin body indicated anything, Addilyn had already suffered.

My guts clenched at the thought that Lloyd might be responsible for her depression and lack of desire to eat, but what else in her cushy life could have caused her to waste away? Certainly not guilt for her part in having me locked up. She'd held her head a little too high that day while striding down the courtroom's aisle. She hadn't even spared me a glance after telling the judge and jury about my behavior. She hadn't reached out to me in those five years either.

The hardness in my stomach overrode the swelling in my jeans, and I clung to the anger. Allowed it to fuel my determination and feed the fire in my head.

For some reason, Addilyn hurt—but she wasn't yet aware of the true meaning of the word pain.

She would be. Soon.

5

Addilyn

Since I no longer participated in social media platforms, I told Ciarra to just give Leo my private cell number to get in touch with me.

He texted within a matter of hours, and we agreed to meet at the pizzeria close to the university. While we shared a couple of classes, I'd never taken note of him, though I never chatted up with anyone who attempted conversation.

I honestly didn't remember who he was—even after Ciarra showed me a picture of him on her Chit'n Chat friends' list.

Cute. Blond hair and hazel eyes.

The guy wasn't intimidating in the least, and his smile suggested he really was the sweetheart Ciarra claimed. I trusted her, and if she'd said he was a good guy, he was.

I hadn't dressed up for our date, hadn't worn

clothing that would attract his gaze or attention. Jeans and a frumpy sweater that hid my thin body and boobs that refused to deflate. Zero makeup as usual—and Ciarra had given me shit for not even adding a touch of blush to make me look less like a corpse.

Baby steps put me in a booth at the restaurant regardless of how I appeared, hands twisting atop my lap while waiting for him.

Another baby step forced a smile on my lips when he showed up a minute later, grinning and flushed.

"Sorry I'm late," he rushed to say while sliding onto the booth across from me.

"I was too."

His grin widened, and he stuck his hand out across the table. "I'm Leo."

Baby step number three included touching his hand rather than eyeing and dismissing him like I usually would have done. No zing of energy like I'd only ever experienced with Gideon raced up my arm as our palms slid together, and I realized I'd secretly been hoping it would.

"Addilyn," I said, praying my disappointment over our lack of connection didn't show on my face.

Obviously a glass half-full type, he oozed an upbeat nature with his permanent smile and the light in his eyes. "So."

I raised an eyebrow.

Chuckling, he leaned forward, his blue eyes rimmed with gold—but they did nothing to my insides like the hooded blue eyes I still dreamed of. "You're beautiful, and I'm the luckiest man alive right now."

Barely holding in my snort, I glanced down at the menu. "Flattery won't get you in my pants."

Nothing would, actually.

"Like most men, I'd rather get you *out* of your pants," he said with another chuckle, "but that's not what I'm here for, Addilyn."

The waitress arrived, drawing Leo's attention off me. "Love your hair," he said to her.

Spikes of purple crowned the waitress's head, odd for a forty-something woman, but whatever floated her boat.

"Thanks." The rasp of her tone indicated a cougar lay waiting to pounce, and her wink solidified the thought in my mind.

As far as I was concerned, they could have each other. While cute, Leo lacked in the areas that turned me on. A rough hand, a commanding presence, and a hint of danger that would send a tingle between my thighs.

He tossed out another compliment—even joked with the woman before she walked away, adding a little extra sway to her hips.

Leo didn't notice. He'd turned back to me.

"Do you always flirt with the waitresses?" I asked, but only to make conversation. Zero trace of jealousy tightened my belly.

"Nah…but my IT buddy did the other night when we went out. Failed miserably—but it wasn't the first time he couldn't connect to the server." Leo waggled his eyebrows, smirking.

It took me a few seconds, but I got it.

A rare, real grin emerged for someone other than Ciarra for the first time since I could remember.

"Ha!" Leo sat back. "I knew you'd have a gorgeous smile."

He turned out to be a decent guy, a jokester who made me almost laugh twice more before our pizza arrived.

Kind like my best friend had stated.

He would never hurt me like I needed to feel arousal though. No sick words like those spewed by Lloyd that my body reacted to regardless of my hatred for him. Leo wouldn't hold me down and fuck me until I bled. Leo wouldn't fist a hand in my hair to keep me still while gagging me with his dick.

A good guy.

Not what my body wanted, unfortunately, even though my mind yearned for such a normal connection. And as that truth evolved and solidified in my mind, I found myself growing quieter. Short one-worded answers about school, studies, plans for the future…all the usual get-to-know-you type shit people conversed about on a first date.

I'd made a mess of the first few I'd attempted throughout the years, and I doubted Leo, even with his sweetness, would end differently. But our failure to find common ground wouldn't be his.

It's me…

"Hey."

I looked up from the slice of pizza I'd managed to mostly eat. Those soft blue eyes flitted over my face.

"You okay?"

"I'm broken," I heard myself spew.

His eyebrows twitched into the first frown I'd seen on his face. "Want to talk about it?"

"Not really," I whispered, shifting on my seat. Silence settled for a few seconds, and I couldn't hold his gaze. The oil atop my pepperoni pizza had coagulated into an orange smear.

My stomach rolled.

"Ciarra told me to not have any expectations," Leo said slowly, as though hoping to not spook me. "It's hard not to with how beautiful you are, how sweet and shy you seem. You're like an onion—in the best way, I mean. All these layers I imagine covering up the diamond inside."

Eyes welling and heart aching, I glanced up, wishing—*wishing*—he imagined correctly. "There's no jewel at my center, Leo. Whatever had been there got crushed years ago."

His lips thinned. "Someone hurt you, didn't they?"

Gratitude for his anger for me, a mere stranger, allowed me to take yet another baby step.

"I could use a friend," I whispered, rather than answering his question.

He flashed a smirk even though I'd rejected him. "Any chance of more down the road?"

"No." I didn't withhold my truth.

"What is it about me that gets me friend-zoned every single time?" Leo asked with a laugh, sitting back with his hands on his thighs. Hardly broken-hearted. Guess he hadn't felt a real connection either.

"You're too kind. Sweet. Sensitive."

"So, you're saying I should let out my darker side?" The waggle of his eyebrows caused something to bubble up inside me, and I found myself laughing lightly. "Pretend I'm some alpha asshole like my sister's book boyfriends?"

"No to all that," I told him, still smiling. "You're perfect just the way you are. Your future partner needs you to complement them."

"You believe in fate, huh?"

I shrugged, my past barreling over me like it always did whenever life allowed me moments of reprieve from depression. Fate had hurt me, but she'd also used me to inflict the same upon others. "Not really, but without at least a grain of hope inside our hearts to clutch onto, what else is there?"

Leo's smile faded as he studied my face. "You cling to that grain, my friend. Don't ever let go."

I nodded, knowing to release my hold on thoughts of a better life would lead to the darkness that had caused Mother to drink and go through men like toilet paper.

A few minutes later, me and my new friend bundled against the cold.

"Can I walk you to your car?" he asked, following me toward the exit.

"You can, but you aren't getting a goodnight kiss," I warned him, proud of myself for lightening up enough to joke.

"I won't try—promise."

That word again...

We stepped out into the night, our breath fogging with the first exhale.

"Shit, it's cold," Leo muttered, hitching his shoulders.

"You really don't have to see me to my car. It's right over there."

"I insist." He bumped my shoulder like Devon used to do in high school—a flirting yet friendly action that brought back a slew of memories.

The boy I'd given my sweet sixteen kiss to.

The one whose bloodied face landed Gideon in jail.

One who'd shunned me after the trial.

If Gideon hadn't been sent away...

A tingle shivered over my skin with a familiarity that caused me to stumble.

Leo grasped my arm. "Okay?" He held onto me until I regained my balance.

"Yeah," I whispered, taking a quick covert glance behind us.

Streetlights, a few cars meandering past, and a handful of people hurrying through the night—nothing out of the ordinary. No dark, lurking shadows waited to swallow me whole.

Leo dropped his hand, and we started forward once more. The closer we got to my car, the more the energy rippling through me kicked up my heart rate. He bumped my arm a second time.

"Are you sure you're alright?"

"Yeah." I studied his smile, suddenly unsure if I could trust him.

With every step, my stomach knotted tighter, and until we reached my car, I trembled, hurrying to get inside. Escape. Shut myself away.

I grabbed the door handle, but Leo lightly touched my forearm. "Hey."

Swallowing, I forced myself to turn and meet his gaze.

"I had a great time tonight—and no, I'm not going to try to kiss you." His wink and grin settled the rising panic inside me that must have been obvious on my face. "But I wouldn't mind hanging out again with you sometime. With Ciarra and her boyfriend if that would make you feel more comfortable."

"I-I'd like that."

"Just shoot me a text when you're ready to peel off another layer, Addilyn." He offered another wink and ambled back across the parking lot, leaving me to watch after his hunched shoulders and quick steps.

Blowing out a breath, I climbed into the car. Hit the locks. Studied the parking lot for the source of that energy I swore licked over my skin—and actually warmed me between the thighs.

It's not my protector, my Gideon.

My body disagreed, the same as it'd been doing for almost two weeks. Scowling, I started up my car and left. I brooded the entire ride home, convincing myself I needed to fall for a guy like Leo.

"Well?" Ciarra asked the second I walked through our front door.

"He's a sweetheart." I pulled off my coat, kicked off my boots, and threw myself onto the couch beside her.

"And?"

"And I friend-zoned him, what else is new?"

Ciarra sighed and tucked me against her side, my head heavy on her shoulder like my heart inside my chest. "I'm proud of you for at least making an effort, Addilyn. It'll get easier with time."

A tear leaked down my cheek at the futility of moving on, and I let it flow.

6

Gideon

The wilted flower went out on a date.

With a blond fucker who looked a little like Devon.

Cold descended over my body while I stood outside the pizzeria in the dark, but I didn't feel the bitter bite. Rage twisted my guts, and I simmered with enough heat to keep my fingers and toes from growing numb.

The prepaid cell I'd bought buzzed in my back pocket, and I dug it out without taking my eyes off of the couple bundling up to head home.

Lloyd: **I'm waiting**

Snarling at the screen, I texted back that he'd be waiting until the time was right. I shut the fucking thing off and stepped into a deeper shadow across the street since the parking area didn't afford me a good view of the restaurant's interior.

Addilyn and the asshole eventually exited, moving across the parking lot together. My stare burned on the back of her head. She stumbled and nearly fell—until the blond fucker touched her.

Fucking touched what didn't belong to him.

Jaw clenched and hands fisting, I roused my self-control to hold still, allowing him to help her right herself, all the while cursing his existence, his smile.

They moved forward once more, and I shifted with the deep darkness of the night, determined to get closer. To stop the fucker from putting his hands on her if he tried.

He bumped her arm a second time, blatantly flirting, and I growled, fingertips itching to rip his face to fucking shreds.

The thought he might kiss her goodnight—or even worse, follow her home to her place, raised my goddamn hackles, and I shivered with the need to unleash some violence. The hunting knife strapped to my waist suddenly felt heavier, the blade seeming to whisper I slid it out into my palm. One slash would spill blood and keep whoever the fucker was from touching her ever again.

From behind a truck, I gritted my teeth and watched them approach her car.

Waited, every cell in my body vibrating.

She went to open her car door, and he reached out for her arm, halting her.

I took a step forward, the handle of the knife in my hand in a blink.

A few mumbled words—and he turned back the way they'd come, sending me sliding into the shadow of the truck.

Addilyn peered after him for a few seconds before climbing inside her car.

I stayed put and pressed against the truck, contemplating the blade in my hand and the clueless fuck seconds from passing me by.

Twinkie had taught me how to wield a knife and where to best stab to end a life.

And I considered it. Fuck, did I think on it.

Saw it in my mind… A quick grab, a single slash across the fucker's throat. The spray of blood reddening the snow and slush at my feet. Soothing my rage's need to unleash.

But he could easily shout before steel met flesh.

And the other people exiting the pizzeria behind me would see.

Five years in prison had been more than enough, and I couldn't afford to land there again without finishing what I had planned.

Pulling back tight against the truck, I held still. Didn't breathe.

And the clueless fuck waltzed right on past, not realizing fate had given him a generous second chance at life.

She had her cup of tea and crawled into bed.

Lights out.

An hour later, Ciarra also slept, and I stood, watching the princess from the hallway, tempted to take—but I hadn't yet gotten Twinkie's supplier to gather what I needed.

I could just knock her ass out and throw her into the back of my Subaru, but my plan involved a mindfuck I refused to give up.

Soon...

She appeared so peaceful burrowed beneath her blankets. So goddamn beautiful, a man could easily get caught up in her poisonous web. I wanted to trail my fingers over her pale skin. Press hard and leave purple bruises or teeth mark indents on her neck. Lick the tears off her sunken cheeks.

Dick throbbing, I eased into her room, my inhales shallow.

Addilyn didn't stir.

Her lips were parted, heavy breaths indicating the chamomile tea she sipped every night afforded her sleep I rarely enjoyed.

Perhaps I need to start drinking that shit.

My balls ached, and I shifted my junk around—but my hand lingered along my shaft. Stroking. Squeezing in time with her soft exhales. That warm, wet mouth...fuck she'd been a sight, peering up at me while I'd fucked over her tongue. Gagging around my length. Tears sludging mascara down her cheeks.

Fuck.

Jaw clenched, I forced my vocal cords to keep quiet and eyed her hamper. The thought of her panties wrapped around my length, the memory of having done so once before, jerked my dick beneath my hand. Yet I couldn't risk the satisfaction of dirtying a pair with my cum and leaving behind evidence.

I eased out of her room before my self-control snapped, and I snuck back up the hallway, walking damn near bow-legged because of my hard-on. The day before, I'd let myself in while the women had been in class, familiarizing myself with the house's entire layout. They rarely visited the basement, so that was where I would sit in wait when the time came.

Two texts showed on my cell once I climbed into my Subaru and powered it back on. One from Lloyd —yet another complaint about having to wait for word that I'd accomplished my job.

The other from Twinkie's contact.

He had the shit I needed.

Grinning, I eyed Addilyn's dark bedroom window.

Tomorrow night, we play.

7

Addilyn

I woke from a dream that Gideon watched over me—protected me in my sleep from Lloyd. Warmth lingered between my thighs, but I ignored my body and climbed from the bed. I hadn't touched myself in years, not since the night before I'd sucked Gideon off.

Climbing into the shower, I allowed myself a moment to reflect on the animalistic nature Gideon had shown when beating on Devon. The blood rage that must have rushed through his veins.

The way he'd ordered me to my knees and told me to suck his dick.

How arousal had owned me and I'd been powerless to do anything but what he'd commanded. He'd looked at me with those wild eyes full of lust and need, the energy between us crackling and whipping into a vortex I couldn't withstand.

He'd gagged me with his cock—and I'd loved it. My panties had soaked through.

But I hadn't felt true satisfaction since.

I let out a heavy, steady exhale and pulled myself back to the present. To the sweet smell of the peach shampoo he'd loved.

Gideon hated me, but did he miss my scent and our banter as much as I did? Did he wonder how things worked out between me and Devon or did he not give a shit after I'd betrayed him?

Devon and Jenny ended up dating a year after Gideon's sentencing while I'd wallowed in misery, shut up in Mother and Lloyd's home. They'd broken up after graduation, and last I'd heard, Devon studied law and planned to run for local office with his father's help. He also had a fiancée from the lower forty-eight.

Jenny had tumbled off the deep end after Devon broke her heart, but the bitch made her bed. She could rot in hell for all I cared.

Her fall to the gutter had come six months earlier —and I'd deleted the two social media accounts I'd kept but rarely visited.

I didn't need to see or hear how everyone else had moved on since my life sucked.

It was why I'd decided to finally claim a major my sophomore year in college—marine biology. Something obscure, something the old me never would've considered. It was the major my best friend studied, so why not?

My grades had suffered those final two years of high school, but Mother's money allowed me entry at the university. Her donations got me into the required classes needed for any degree.

And now with her gifts, loving or otherwise, dried up…

The lawyer returned my call in the afternoon. Lloyd had no ground to stand on in any attempt to claim my inheritance. Yes, he could keep me from drawing on it until my twenty-first birthday in less than two months, but I didn't yet have need of the cash. Both credit cards she'd given me had been deactivated—I'd learned that while attempting to get groceries two days after her death—but I had a small savings of my own.

Enough for two months of bills. Enough to see me through to my birthday.

Lloyd wasn't a patient man when it came to getting what he wanted. Had he planned to make me sorry for denying him like he'd claimed, he would have made an attempt already. My mind eased up enough that I managed to eat an entire bowl of soup for dinner.

Leo had texted, inviting me out with him and his friends, but I declined.

Ciarra and her boyfriend left for their usual

Friday date night for dinner and dancing at a club in downtown Anchorage.

I sat home, alone. The windows and doors were locked up tight. The TV formed a buzzing backdrop while I put the kettle on for my tea. After a quick trip to my bedroom for my sleep shirt and robe, I returned to find the water steaming.

Tea mug in hand, I settled onto the couch with a throw blanket, letting out a heavy exhale.

Nothing better than a quiet night in with my e-reader.

Within minutes, I lost myself in the virtual pages, and all thoughts of reality and life fled from my mind.

Barely eight-thirty and my eyelids drooped, the words in front of my eyes wavering. Exhaustion sank into my bones, and I groaned at the thought that I had to get up and go to bed.

I shivered, coolness sliding over my neck as I forced myself to sit. Dizziness swarmed over me, and I blinked the TV into focus.

A news anchor waved at the green screen behind him depicting the map with an incoming storm heading our way. We would probably wake to a few feet of snow.

Yawning, I clicked off the TV and stood.

My equilibrium hiccupped, and I grabbed hold of the couch's arm.

"Shit."

Had I spiked my own damn tea without remembering?

Just tired. Exhausted emotionally and mentally.

I needed my bed.

Not wanting to leave a mess for Ciarra, I managed to refold my blanket and put my mug in the dishwasher.

Jaw cracking with a yawn, I shuffled back the hallway, intent on my pillow.

The softness of cotton and feathers caressed my cheek, and I sighed, sinking down into darkness.

8

Gideon

I waited in the pitch black, listening to the footsteps overhead and the murmurs of the two friends. My legs grew restless as I sat beside a stack of bins, knees drawn up, arms resting atop them. My head tipped back against the wall behind me. My eyes remained wide open, unseeing through the same black as my soul.

A similar pose I'd spent hours in during those days of solitary…

Pushing aside thoughts of prison, I focused on the footfalls tracking across above me. The shower running. Silence for a time.

More murmurs.

The front door closed as Ciarra left for her Friday night date, same as the previous two weeks.

Addilyn stayed in, alone.

Time to play.

Grinning, I stayed put for a few moments longer, my plan ready to roll thanks to Twinkie's dealer.

I just needed to get the crushed pill into Addilyn's tea water which wouldn't prove difficult. The woman was a creature of habit to a fault.

An hour after Ciarra left, I listened to my prey cross the kitchen floor overhead. The sink's spigot turned on, and I envisioned Addilyn filling her tea kettle with fresh water as usual.

I eased up from my position and used a small flashlight to make my way toward the basement stairs.

Addilyn's steps took her back through the hallway into the bathroom where she would change into that thin, blue T-shirt she always wore to bed—and I sprinted on socked feet up the stairs into the kitchen. Adrenaline coursed through me, but my hand held steady while emptying out some of the water from the kettle for potency's sake before dropping the powder in.

I set it back on the stove and slipped down to the basement again, my pulse thrumming.

Addilyn moved around the house, and I gave her a good fifteen minutes before sneaking up the stairs again. With the door cracked open, I watched as the back of her head settled against the couch's arm, my heart thumping in my ears.

She read on an e-reader, the TV on the other side of the room flickering, its volume down near zero.

Still awake…

Would she realize she'd been drugged? If so, I expected she'd text Ciarra—something I couldn't allow. If she made any move for the cell I could see on the end table, I would have no choice but to walk in and take her, consciousness be damned.

I hoped for her to pass out, clueless, only to wake as my captive.

She set the reading device aside after close to a half hour or so and turned off the TV, her upper body swaying.

She continued to weave as she stood, and a soft curse left her as she grasped at the couch. Frowning, she attempted to fold a blanket, and she moved like a drunken sailor while taking her tea mug to the kitchen.

She rinsed it and into the dishwasher it went.

Perfect.

Shuffled footsteps took her back the hallway, and I let myself into the kitchen, trailing along silently after her in my socks.

Ciarra wouldn't be home for at least three hours…plenty of time to execute what I'd been planning.

Addilyn went down face first onto her mattress, and I grinned from her bedroom doorway, my blood flooding with a fresh burst of need. I returned to the living room where she'd left her cell.

Texted Ciarra.

I'm exhausted, I typed out. **Sleeping in tomorrow, so don't wake me before noon.**

After good wipe down, I placed her cell on her bedstand.

Ciarra's reply came through before the screen shut off. **Sweet dreams.**

My snort didn't rouse Addilyn.

Neither did my touch to her hip and shoulder as I pushed her onto her back.

Her robe gaped open, revealing the same T-shirt she always wore to bed. Blue and faded. Worn out in a few places.

The damn thing looked familiar…

White cotton panties peeked from beneath the hem—right at the apex of her splayed thighs.

My dick went from chub to full on ready to fuck, and I reached out to run a fingertip along the top of her thigh—back and forth beneath the shirt's hem. Slowly lifting, pushing the soft material higher toward her hip.

Revealing her panties fully and sending a jolt of lust through my dick.

Pre-cum oozed at the thought of the pussy I'd dreamed of owning. Wet and hot. Tight and pink. Fucking delicious if the scent of her panties I'd taken all those years ago was any indication.

Swallowing drool, I pushed the shirt higher, my palm sliding up her side until her pert tit was uncovered.

Fuck. Me.

She'd lost a shit ton of weight, but her rack…

I shoved the shirt up to her neck and stepped back. Hip bones and ribs poked out under her pale skin. But those tits.

Teeth clenched, I palmed my dick and squeezed.

Fuck, how I wanted to do more than touch. I lusted to shove into her tight body and ride the fuck out of it until I exploded.

But she wouldn't know.

Wouldn't remember.

There wouldn't be pain and tears.

And those things I needed to take from her.

I pulled out my cock and gave it a few good, hard tugs before deciding on the best way to ease the ache in my balls.

Fingers tucked beneath those virginal panties, I slid them down, right off her limp legs. Then I splayed those thighs wide open and drank in her beauty. Pink pussy. Fucking pale blonde hair—fuck, I had dreamed about what I'd find.

Mystery solved—a true blonde regardless of her dark eyelashes and brows.

"Fuck, princess." I wrapped her panties around my dick, groaning at the lingering warmth of the cotton. I eyed the smooth folds of her pussy, the little nub at the top, and the dark crevice leading to her ass I couldn't wait to claim.

Two strokes and my cum shot into her panties,

my hips jerking and my hand squeezing and milking. My nostrils flared with every grunted exhale.

She didn't move through it all.

Chest heaving, I gathered my cum in the wrecked panties, shoved them into my pocket, and yanked my zipper up. I'd claimed relief enough to get my prize back to Twinkie's cabin that I'd prepared over the previous couple of days.

A place where no one would think to look, deep in the Alaskan wilderness, a shack that sat warm and stocked for a good two months' worth of hiding out.

Lloyd would get his wish for Addilyn to disappear, but I had no intention of letting him see her ever again. She would be my prisoner until her twenty-first birthday.

I would have my revenge on the fucker who spawned me, his friend the sheriff, and even Devon.

Then, I would decide Addilyn's fate.

A man needed money to live—perhaps I would allow the princess to ransom her own life with the inheritance she'd have access to within a short matter of weeks.

But first, I would make her pay for her betrayal.

My fucking dick twitched again at the thought, but I ignored the rekindled lust and set to work bundling up my captive for the long ride ahead of us.

9

Addilyn

Muscles heavy and aching, I groaned as I woke, keeping my eyelids clenched tight.

Did I get run over by a truck?

My brain seemed swelled inside my skull, throbbing, threatening to liquify and leak out my ears.

"Shit," I muttered and tried to roll into a fetal position.

I couldn't move. Couldn't blink open my eyes.

Black. Blindfold.

"What—" A harsh pull on my arms as I woke fully tightened the ties around my wrists, and I hissed, yanking again, hard enough that my joints hurt. My chest tightened. I didn't need to pinch myself to know I wasn't dreaming.

My legs—

Oh fuck...

My stomach rolled, and I swallowed hard, attempting to move my legs again. Tied up. Spread open. Ankles cuffed, same as my wrists.

Oh fuck, oh fuck, oh fuck...

Voice catching on a sob, I yanked again, but my binds held firm.

Adrenaline crashed through me, easing my muscle aches, and my heartbeat thundered in my ears.

I'd had fantasies of being kidnapped and restrained, but the reality settled in, panic demanding I flee.

"Help me!" I shrieked and choked on a breath, my rising terror uncaring as to who would hear—Lloyd, someone random—I just needed out. Freedom. I shifted my head on the pillow to dislocate my blindfold. "Please! Somebody!"

Thrashing only chafed my wrists and ankles, and I gulped a few times, hoping to relieve the tightness in my chest. The panic stole my breath and heated my body to the point of sweat.

Calm down. Use your brain...

No one touched me. Nothing made a sound beyond the pulse of rushing blood in my ears. I tried to lie still, panting and shuddering involuntarily. Shivering even though I burned up.

No air caressed my skin—I still wore Gideon's shirt that had replaced my sleep shorts and camisoles from years earlier. Threadbare and worn, it was a comfort when I woke from my nightmares.

This is no nightmare.

I whimpered, lightheaded from a lack of oxygen in my squeezing lungs. "H-hello? P-Please...let mm-e go. Please."

Softness cradled my entire backside rather than a hard surface like dirt or cement. The air didn't reek of decay or a damp cellar. Heaviness like a blanket lay atop most of my body.

Shit could be worse, I tried telling myself over and over, but nothing calmed my racing heart or the adrenaline continuing to pour into my blood.

Think...

Lloyd hadn't ever restrained me in such a fashion, spread eagle on top of what had to be a bed. I took stock of my body from my throbbing temples down to my toes...and found no soreness between my thighs, no ache from having been assaulted while unconscious, but...

Tingles worked through my core, a warmth where none ought to be in a healthy woman's mind as memories flashed through my mind of being forced to comply...used in my inability to fight.

Sick, I'm so damn sick.

I gulped, forcing my mind away from my unwanted arousal. How could my body panic and get turned on at the same time? Had Lloyd fucked me up so badly that my body craved the fear? The pain he would bring?

I didn't *want* it. Hated it, hated him.

Whoever it was must have drugged me—not Lloyd. No, Lloyd would have taken advantage of me while I'd been unconscious. He'd done so before…

Someone else had been in my house. Or was I *still* in my house?

Ears straining, I listened for the sounds of cars driving by, voices, a TV or radio…anything.

Nothing.

Dead silence like I'd been tied up in a tomb.

I'm in a bed. It's warm—no tomb.

Focusing on breathing, I managed to calm my adrenal glands and ease the tight vise around my chest enough so I didn't wheeze for breath. But my body continued its sick want, the growing throb between my thighs making me pull against my restraints to try and close them.

My eyes stung and spilled, but the tears had no escape. Slowly, they absorbed into my blindfold, and I bit my lip to keep from sobbing.

Don't break, Addilyn Jane. Don't break. Be strong.

The pep talk continued in my head for a few minutes, calming my heart rate as my tears dried. Eventually, I breathed evenly. Clear headed.

After living under Lloyd, giving into fear wasn't an option. It was what he'd lusted after. I'd escaped him once, and if that's who had captured me, I would do so again.

Or die trying.

A squeak sounded…a door opening?

I held my breath, lifting my head off the pillow, desperate to see beyond the blackness.

My skin pebbled like an electrical charge rushed through me.

Gideon.

Longing for him to rescue me, to protect me, stabbed me in the chest harshly enough that I bit back a sob, knowing the futility of my thoughts.

He sat in jail because of me, and I would have to look after myself, same as I'd done before.

Footsteps—I held my breath again, tensing and bracing myself for an unwanted touch, ready to fight until my body gave out.

Clothing shifted. Another creak, the sounds of… someone sitting on a cushion?

Turning my head, I faced whoever had joined me. "What do you want?" I asked past the tightness in my throat threatening to choke me. "If it's money, I've got lots of it."

Well, I would in a few weeks.

Whoever I felt staring at me didn't answer.

I reached out with my senses, desperate to learn all I could about the person who'd kidnapped me. The more I knew, the better my chances of survival and eventual escape would be.

Woodsmoke scented the air.

Hollow-sounding breathing like one would make through a mask reached my ears.

A scrape, like a shoe scuffing on flooring.

My skin pebbled again as though he watched me. Studied me. Same as Gideon had always done. Wanting.

"Don't look at me," I whispered at the captor I feared to be Lloyd without meaning to voice my weak thoughts. My breath grew ragged at knowing how my body would react. *Don't look at me—don't want me. Please.*

The warmth between my thighs intensified, and I swallowed hard against renewed tears. I could control my mind, my panic—but not my damn body.

So sick.

Lloyd's fault.

I focused on that truth and blamed him for my body's unwanted reaction. Fantasies of my youth had been just that—fantasy. No sane or normal person really wished to be kidnapped, tied up, and used.

His fault.

Memories of his touch, his taking, caused heat to rise in my belly, the kind that demanded I scream and attempt to break free. Fight to defend an innocence already stolen. More adrenaline released regardless of my struggle to remain strong and calm, and I pulled against my restraints.

No, no, no...

My breath caught on a sob as I wrenched my arms, desperate to break my bonds.

The pain in my joints and futility of my movements only intensified my anger and fear, my muscles quivering uncontrollably.

"Let me go!" I shrieked, yanking and thrashing, all trace of aches in my body fading in the need to escape. "Let me go!"

Tightness grew in my chest until I gasped for air, my movements jerky. Lessening as darkness crept in my periphery.

My ragged inhales echoed in my ears along with the steady thumps of my heartbeat. Guess I didn't have as great control as I'd thought.

I'm dying...oh god, I'm dying...

10

Gideon

She fought like a wildcat, her growing panic making my dick hard. Her shrieks caused blood to rush through my veins, and I gripped the chair's arms where I sat on the opposite side of the cabin's lone bedroom so I wouldn't grab my throbbing length.

Pre-cum oozed from my slit, smearing inside my jeans, and still, I didn't touch myself.

I fucking gloried in watching the little bitch gasp for oxygen and tremble with fear over the reality of what she'd fantasized about as a teenager.

The quilt I'd covered her with lay askew, and the T-shirt rose up her spread thighs, revealing the thatch of blonde hair at her core and the pink petals of her pussy…

Fuck.

Mouth drooling, I studied how she shivered, how

her muscles quivered. Her tits jiggled with every attempt at escape.

I stared, soaking in her cries. Getting off on her weakness of being at my mercy. While I could have gone with zip ties to bind her, I wasn't ready yet for blood. Soft hemp rope tied her ankles and wrists to the lone bed, allowing her as much comfort as possible in her situation.

But not me.

My groin ached, and inside the gas mask with its mesh holes for the eyes and mouth, my breathing heightened, making me sound like a real-life Darth Vader. Jaw clenched, I sat like a statue, sucking oxygen through my flared nostrils. I was tensed tight as fuck down to my marrow, the pain, the lust to take from her all-consuming.

The need for something beyond my hand—fucking six years' worth—drew my balls up, ready to explode.

But my self-control held. Minutes ticked by.

Addilyn's demands to be untied, to be released, for me to stop watching her eventually quieted. Her fight to escape slowed until all that remained were involuntary muscle spasms. Twitches of instinct as her mind shut down but her body continued its drive for freedom.

Shivers across her skin.

Goosebumps rising as though I trailed my fingers up her thigh.

Silence settled over us, the tension thick with arousal and terror.

"Let me go," she whispered again, a shudder rippling down over her.

Never.

Not nearly having my fill of her fear, I stood, ready to play some more.

Her head jerked my way as though she noticed the soft rustle of my clothing. "D-Don't touch me..."

How many times had she said that to me in the past when I'd pressed her against doors, letting her feel the hardness of my want for her? Hearing her say it again after five years made my dick dribble pre-cum.

I adjusted my bulge, squeezing a bit at the base of my length while approaching the bed. Her blindfold hadn't moved, but I kept my mask on, not willing to take a chance of her identifying me.

She shivered. Her skin popped with goosebumps again from head to toe.

I pulled the quilt fully off her trembling form and climbed onto the bed.

"Don't," she stated through gritted teeth as though finding some strength deep inside her.

Heart racing, I straddled her thighs, and she stilled completely. Chest not rising—but she gasped as I placed my palm on her lower belly where pale skin peeked from beneath her shirt's hem.

Soft as fuck—making me harder than steel.

"D-Don't." Not sounding so confident with that tremor in her voice.

I grinned, adrenaline and the need for well-earned, well-deserved release rushing through me like a goddamn tsunami hellbent on reaching land.

Inch by inch, I slid my palm beneath the shirt and up her torso, over her prominent breastbone and between her suddenly heaving tits. I closed my hand around her neck and took off my mask, setting it aside since she lay powerless beneath my hold.

The rich princess trembled, her full lips parted as she panted, and the pulse beneath my fingertips grew rapid as fuck.

Hyperventilation lay seconds away—but I grasped her hair and yanked her head back, exposing her throat. Leaning down, I tightened my hold on her neck, cutting off her air and pulling strands of her shorter hair from her scalp at the same time.

Her whimper—fucking fuel to my lust.

I slid my nose along the satiny skin beneath her ear. Beneath the stench of her terror hinted at sweet peaches.

Memories of sniffing after her like a dog rose, and my dick jerked in its prison. I bit back a groan, my grasp on her neck unrelenting as my self-control wavered.

I needed to hurt her.

Her pulse weakened, and she didn't make a sound. Without a doubt, couldn't. I licked along her jaw line, tasting the salt of her sweat while choking her out. Her scent, the flavor of her fear consumed my senses, taking me past the breaking point.

She didn't fight me though. I'd wanted her thrashing, begging, crying…

Addilyn's body went limp.

I jerked my hand away from her neck, sitting back and scowling at the unmoving woman before me spread out like a goddamn feast for a starved animal like me.

The fuck had I done? I had no intention of taking her past the point of resisting.

Her pulse still beat in her neck though…

I could fuck her awake. Shove my dick so far up her pussy she came to with a shriek. The idea jerked my already strangled dick in my jeans, but I clenched my jaw and fists, needing to keep control rather than ravage.

Not on day one, I told myself.

I had too much fear to inflict before having what I'd been thinking about.

But that didn't mean I couldn't find my release and leave her with the evidence. That would definitely ring on panic once she woke and realized what I'd done.

I rose onto my knees and pulled my dick out, palming my throbbing length while staring at her body—the fluttering pulse in her neck, the parted lips.

Fuck, she was beautiful.

Tugging on my dick, I soaked the rest of her in.

Dark pink nipples I salivated to taste. The hollow of her belly. Pale pubic hair, the nub beneath laid bare from her tied-open thighs. Soft petals…glistening wetness…

The fuck?

Dropping my hold on my aching length, I leaned down and rubbed my nose over the soft curls between her legs. Womanly musk filled my senses, my lungs as I inhaled, making my dick leak.

Well, fuck me.

The naughty bitch *did* get off on being tied up, on being taken against her will. No wonder she'd stilled when I'd straddled her thighs before choking her to unconsciousness—she'd been giving me the goddamn green light to take what I wanted.

Fuck.

I grabbed my dick again, squeezing to the point of pain to keep from stabbing it into her. My fist would do until I had my share of causing the poised princess to buckle to fear.

She whimpered, rousing, and I straightened, the schlicking noise of me fucking my fist rising between us. I imagined her pussy sucking me deep into her body. Strangling my dick.

The wet sound of me jerking off couldn't be mistaken for anything other than what it was, but she didn't scream or attempt to escape while coming to.

Addilyn gasped and stopped moving. Tensed. Her nipples hardened beneath my stare. The pulse in her neck throbbed.

And I'd thought she was so damn smart. Stupid, stupid girl, allowing her fantasies to dictate her future.

She shifted her hips as though needing me, every inch of my length she'd once gagged around. I could finger her tight little hole, and she would probably moan rather than tell me to fuck off. I could probably fuck into her puckered rosebud, and she wouldn't fight.

I didn't want her orgasms.

I didn't want her cum.

I wanted her tears.

My balls tingled, and a deep groan rose from my chest as I fucked my fist faster—harder—needing to scare the shit out of her by painting her body with hot spurts of milky white.

Addilyn's breath held as though she too stood on the brink of ecstasy.

Spunk shot up through my length, ribboning across her belly. I bit into my tongue, tasting copper to keep from uttering a spew of curses or any sound she might recognize.

A shudder rippled over her body, once more bringing goosebumps across her skin.

Teeth clenched and sucking air through my nose, I caught the final dribble of cum in my palm.

Moisture lined her pink slit.

Damn woman had gotten turned on over my seed shooting across her skin. I scowled harder, deeper as I realized a part of me loved her response to my hate. Addilyn didn't lie tied to the bed for her own pleasure. She was at my mercy. Mine. For revenge, for *my* satisfaction.

Suddenly needing space, I stood and left her alone. Let my markings stay where they'd smeared.

Time to get my head on fucking straight and take things to a new level.

11

Addilyn

He'd choked me out and jerked off all over my stomach—hitting every single one of my body's arousal buttons.

Sick fucks, both of us.

He could have raped me...

I lay still, my face hot with shame, my captor's energy gone from the room. Silence once more reigned while I slowly calmed, my arousal waning. I should have freaked the fuck out. Heart racing, stomach heaving, same as whenever Lloyd had taken from me.

My brow furrowed beneath my blindfold.

A sense of...security...lay impossibly deep inside my bones.

I couldn't out figure my body's reaction to his hand, his cum cooling on my stomach. Even though the lack of fear troubled me, I let it rest. Waiting...

for what, I had no clue. His cum dried on my skin, creating an itch I couldn't relieve.

I wallowed in my body's traitorous instincts to fuck rather than fight. I could have attempted to headbutt him even though he'd held my hair to the point my scalp stung. I could have turned my face and tried to bite the tongue licking along my jaw— but I reasoned my passivity away with the darkness infringing on my consciousness from his harsh grip on my throat.

Then I'd come to.

And my body literally sang at the wet noises he made jerking off, same as that time I'd watched Gideon with my panties.

The hint of a grunt passing his lips, the wet heat splattering over my belly had been ten times better than the fantasy I'd had of Gideon finishing all those years ago.

Frowning over my renewing arousal, I turned my thoughts onto things that would bring back the desire to fight for freedom like a strong, *sane* woman ought to do.

I doubted my kidnapping was coincidence when Lloyd promised me I would pay for kicking him in the balls and refusing to give in to his demands to become his willing lover.

Lloyd would be coming to claim me from the man he must have hired to grab me—and unlike my captor, he would have his way regardless of my consent.

The man who'd lifted my shirt and ran his hand clear up to my throat hadn't squeezed my breasts. Hadn't stroked between my thighs even though they'd been held spread open for the taking.

And there was no way he hadn't noticed the wetness coating me down there.

But how long would his self-control withstand a bound woman and his obvious lust if the many stripes of dried cum pulling at my skin was any indication? And would I really fight him off if he attempted more?

My brain said yes.

My body yearned for his touch.

A well-meaning, nice guy like Leo couldn't rouse an ounce of desire in my blood, but a man I knew would take without asking could?

I'd lied to myself when denying I'd wanted Gideon all those years ago.

I didn't lie to myself about not wanting his father.

And yet they both brought on my body's desire to be filled—one with outright lust, the other with the pain he'd inflicted.

Sick.

Heat rushed to my face, and I wished to sink into the mattress, to disappear forever.

I needed to find a new therapist in the worst way —if I ever made it out of my predicament alive.

You're getting out of here.

But how? When? Without knowing anything about who had kidnapped me or where he held me, I couldn't form a plan of escape.

Letting out a heavy, slow exhale, I focused on relaxing. Conserving my energy. My mind quieted in the stillness that seemed to go on for hours, my muscles eventually giving in to exhaustion.

I woke with a jolt, limbs jerking. I was still bound, blindfolded, and desperate for a bathroom, but the panic had severely lessened from the first time I'd woken in my captor's bed.

How long had I slept?

Tingles slid over my body, heating my skin. Even without seeing or hearing, I recognized the energy in the room as the same from earlier, the same as when I'd felt sure someone followed me and Ciarra.

Whoever it was, he'd been stalking me for days.

My captor watched—if only it was my protector who hated me rather than the asshole who'd taken me from my bed. Longing for Gideon tightened my throat, but it wasn't his nearness I felt like a whispered breeze, a lick of energy over my skin that lit up every atom in my body.

Warmth.

Swelling.

Need rose inside me, and I couldn't lay still from arousal and self-hatred at my body's reaction. I shifted, making me once more aware of the fullness of my bladder.

I licked my lower lip, realizing I had no moisture left in my mouth. "I have to pee," I croaked out.

He didn't speak, but I didn't doubt his presence—whoever the hell he was.

"I have to pee," I stated louder, firmly enough that he couldn't mistake my seriousness.

Silence stretched until I gritted my teeth.

"Do you want me to wet this bed? Soak the sheets? I have to *pee*!"

With a rustle of clothing, I felt him draw nearer.

Cold metal scraped up the inside of my leg, stinging yet not cutting.

A knife.

My breath caught on a gasp as my skin broke into goosebumps.

The scratch deepened along the inside of my thigh, and I bit my lip against the pain, the sure welling of blood.

The fucker had cut me.

And being the sick fuck I was, I liked it. Pulsed for more.

"Any sudden movements, and I'll slice you to shit." He sounded dead, a hollow tone as though speaking through a mask.

A shudder rippled over me, and I nodded, telling

myself knife play wasn't my kink, that my brain was still messed up from whatever drug he'd given me.

The restraints around my ankles loosened, and I whimpered while trying to pull my thighs together. My hips ached, my joints on fire.

Even worse, I couldn't shift my arms once he released them. He grasped my wrist and yanked me toward the bed's edge, pulling me up and back against him, my arm twisted between us.

Weakness plagued my legs, but he held me against hard, hot muscle.

Bigger—stronger—a beast of a man.

Not my Gideon.

My throat tightened as I released that tiny seed of hope I'd held onto deep inside my heart. I refused the tears that wanted to leak from my eyes and soak my blindfold with every step he half-carried, half-dragged me.

Warmer air licked at my skin. Crackle of a fire. Wind. The sound of ice-like snow pinging windows.

A storm had moved in.

I'd been gone for at least twelve hours, according to the weather report I'd watched before passing out at home—if we were even still in the Anchorage area.

My captor spun me, lowering me by my armpits —toilet.

Thank god.

Arms still aching from being tied overhead, I

tenderly gathered the hem of my old shirt around my waist, uncaring of my nudity—he'd seen it all. He'd covered my skin with cum.

I hated the tingle between my thighs over the thought.

My bladder relaxed, and I let out a shuddered sigh, swaying on the hard seat.

Water ran, but I couldn't be bothered with what he did as my body found relief in a slow dribble, indicating I'd been holding my urine for far too long. With the ease of my bladder came the next item on my to-do list. Find out who he was and where we were so I could plan how to escape him.

Finally finished, I sat and waited. Spine as stiff as it could be, considering my aching body. Chin held high, even though I couldn't see a damn thing from behind my blindfold.

The temptation to rip the material off my face itched my fingers, but he held a knife and had said I wasn't to make any sudden movements.

I was smart enough to obey—for a time.

"Stand."

I attempted to do as I was told, stumbling—he grasped my upper arm, fingers digging in and without doubt marking my skin. So, he no longer held the knife in his right hand.

A warm, wet towel slapped into my other hand.

He'd given me something to clean myself. Why do so if he intended me real harm?

"Who are you?" I asked.

"No one that matters," he grunted the words with his dead voice.

Slowly, so he wouldn't freak out and slash me with the knife he'd put who the hell knew where, I wiped between my thighs. I folded the warm towel in half and rubbed beneath the shirt, attempting to rid myself of his dried cum.

He yanked my hand from beneath my covering, ripping the towel from me.

"That stays."

Sick arousal rose between my thighs at how he wanted his scent, his mark to remain on me.

But I focused on the bruising grip on my arm I needed to break free from as he led me away from the bathroom.

No more hollowed-out words, just the sounds of Mother Nature accompanied our slow trek back to my cell of sorts as I wracked my brain, soaking in the details of what lay around us.

Hardwood floor beneath my bare feet. The warmth of a fireplace that let out a loud pop of sparks.

"Where are we?" I asked, my voice steadier than I'd expected.

He didn't reply.

"It's still snowing?"

I didn't get a verbal response.

The scent of toast teased my nose.

"I'm hungry," I said, knowing I would need sustenance for whatever escape I attempted in the hopefully near future.

He once more spun me, and the mattress hit the back of my legs.

I sat and stayed put—wasn't about to lay down and let him tie me up again.

"I'm hungry," I stated again, chin lifting as though I could see him through my blindfold.

The door closed. A lock clicked.

I held my breath, but no rustle of clothing met my straining ears, and no tingling awareness of his presence ghosted over my skin

Had he left me alone without restraints?

My hands shook as I clutched the sheet beside my thighs. Did I dare?

My pulse pounding, adrenaline leaking into my bloodstream, I decided to go for it.

I raised my hand slow as hell, giving him plenty of time to tell me to stop if he still sat in the room with me, but no such command followed. I peeled the blindfold up—and found myself in pitch black.

Curses rang between my ears, but I took the moment's freedom, pushing up onto weak legs. I felt along the edge of the bed, around the foot, and up the other side. Met a log wall with my fingertips. I trailed my left hand at window height along the bumpy surface, keeping the other one in front of me, ready for obstacles.

A corner.

Three steps in and my shin bashed against the chair, the one he must have watched me from.

Around the chair—door.

My breath held. I tried the handle, but it didn't give.

Continuing my walk eventually put me back at the bed's side, my adjusted eyes still not able to see a damn thing.

One bed, one chair. One locked door, and no window.

The lack of light bothered me the most, but I curled up on the bed beneath the lone quilt and closed my eyes to block that truth out, pretending I had my nightlight plugged in beside me.

Hunger twisted my stomach, but at least I lay in warmth, no longer tied up and unable to move.

Worry began to eat at my mind with the thought of Lloyd's imminent arrival, but I forced it from my head, refusing to break for him ever again.

Exhaustion and weakness took over.

True darkness swept me away to where neither existed any longer.

I dreamed of kneeling at Gideon's feet. Peering up at him, worshiping him as he stared down at me with his lust-filled, hooded gaze that made me wet.

Blinding light brought me to reality, and I gasped, shielding my stinging eyes and scrambling against the headboard.

Squinting and blinking barely allowed me time to make out a beast dressed in all black—well over six feet of solid muscle beneath his tight, long-sleeved shirt. A gas mask of sorts with mesh over the eyes covered his head fully. No hint of hair, no glimpse of eye color.

Nothing leading to his identity whatsoever.

He set a tray on the chair and stalked back out, shutting the door behind him.

Leaving me in a brightly lit room.

The scent of eggs and toast wafted my way—and I scooted off the bed without another thought than filling the emptiness in my stomach.

No utensils—but I didn't care. I shoveled that shit into my mouth with my fingers, zero trace of manners in mind, not giving two shits that I hadn't washed my hands after peeing earlier.

Warm eggs, scrambled and cooked to perfection. Lightly buttered toast, the perfect amount of crunch —exactly how I liked it.

Tea.

Chamomile *freaking* tea.

My throat swelled, even as a tingle slid down my spine over the slap of truth. He'd been watching me long enough to know it was my drink of choice.

I let the mug sit, still steaming, while I sucked

down the water and wiped out the meal he'd left for me.

My stomach ached from scarfing down the food, but I took the tea in my trembling hands and sat once more against the headboard. My knees were drawn up, T-shirt stretched out and over them to my ankles.

He'd fed me—he intended to keep me alive.

Hopefulness once more rose inside my breast, and I clung to the flutter in my belly, telling myself I could face Lloyd again when the time came. I would eat every bit of food my captor brought me in preparation to fight. I would feign being broken in submission to draw Lloyd close—and I would find a way to hurt him. To show him he would never control me and he would never have me again.

Breathing out a heavy exhale, I examined my room.

Log walls like I'd felt with my fingertips, the lone chair with the empty tray, and the bed I sat upon. One light with its blinding bulb hung overhead.

And a small camera up in the far corner faced toward me.

Even when not in the room with me, he watched.

Of course he did.

Hours passed, at least what felt like it, while I sat in silence, sipping my cooling tea. My mind was full of more questions than answers. Without a window,

I had no way to tell time, but it wouldn't have mattered.

I had nothing to do but wait and try to not over-think my situation or put myself into a panic. While powerless over my circumstances, I could manage myself.

My bladder and bowels, however, had a mind of their own, but my captor didn't return for the tray.

It felt silly to knock on my locked door, but what choice did I have? Leave a puddle and a pile of shit in the corner like a desperate puppy?

I knocked. "Hello?"

No answer, no sound came from whatever lay outside my room.

"Hello?" I hollered and faced the camera, my palm hitting the oak door rather than my knuckles. "I need to use the bathroom again!"

Still nothing.

Did he want me shitting on the floor?

I lifted my hand, ready to scream—and the door jerked open.

He loomed over me, the mask black and scary as fuck—more so than the blade held beneath my nose.

"Bathroom," I demanded, shivering under the gaze of the mesh-covered eyes I swore devoured me.

Grasping my upper arm to the point of bruising, he once more half-dragged me across a small, open-concept room with log walls like the bedroom where he kept me.

Two windows flanked a front door, both showing a swirl of white, a shed a short ways away, and nothing else.

It still snowed.

Fireplace. Two cabinets. A small kitchen table. A book on the end table by a threadbare couch. A pillow and two blankets revealed where he slept—he'd shoved me into a smaller room.

Bathroom.

I stumbled on my own to the toilet, pulled up my shirt, and sank down on the seat, letting out a sigh, not having a single fuck to give over the fact he watched. Eyes closed, I relaxed and let my body do its thing.

Once I finished and wiped with the roll of toilet paper hanging on the wall beside me, I stood, my shirt falling midthigh to cover my nakedness. Only then did I lift my focus off the combat boots in front of me.

Black jeans covered his long legs and powerful thighs—and the type of bulge a woman in my situation shouldn't find herself drooling over. His tight black shirt encased prominent pectorals, protruding shoulder and bicep muscles, and it covered his thick forearms, ending at his wrists.

But the mask…

I gulped, turning my focus to the small shower stall on my left. "C-Can I shower?" I asked, hating that my voice betrayed my quaking insides.

"No." He pointed toward the small living area.

I slipped past him without looking at his masked face, my gaze latching on the window filled with white. The door beside it didn't have a deadbolt or chain. A simple lock…

My pulse stumbled then sped as I recognized the fact I had an opportunity.

A battery-operated lamp sat on the small table I approached—and my captor breathed on my neck.

I slowed, sucking oxygen into my lungs.

You can do this. Do it!

I grabbed the lamp and swung around.

My kidnapper's head was tilted down like he'd been checking out my ass—and I clobbered him in the temple. He stumbled, but I didn't hang around to see if he fell. Heart racing, I took off for the door.

"Fuck!" he groaned, but no crashing sound announced that I'd hit him hard enough to drop him to his knees.

My shaking fingers flicked the lock, and I pulled the door inward.

Frigid air blasted my face, stole my breath.

"Run," he whispered close to my ear—and I sprinted into the blinding white.

12

Gideon

The ballsy bitch hit me hard enough to knock my mask askew, and my goddamn ear rang, but I didn't reach out to grab her. Rage rose, stirring my blood, the same that wet my fingertips when I touched them to my temple before righting my mask.

She scampered toward the door like she thought she could escape me. Escape the cabin deep in the wilderness, far from civilization—and in the middle of a snowstorm.

Stupid girl.

Guess she hadn't smartened up while I'd been away.

Three quiet strides put me inches from her ass as she wrenched the door open, but I held my fists at my sides rather than taking her down like I lusted to do.

"Run," I whispered harshly, inches from her ear.

Her shriek caused satisfaction to swell inside me, chubbed my dick, and I grinned like a maniac as she ran out into the storm.

Bare fucking feet. Nothing but a T-shirt covering her thin body.

She wouldn't get far, but I would give her a good enough head start to fill me with an even greater sense of satisfaction when I hunted down my prey. Allowing her feel hope. Catching the little princess. Listening to her pleading to let her go. She'd attempt to bribe me, something she'd been too weak to do up to that point.

I would break her rigid spine, rip that hope to shreds, and tear her down to a sobbing, begging mess.

My dick hopped aboard that fucking train of demolition. Not bothering to grab a coat, I shut the cabin door behind me. My mask kept the dying eddies of the wind away, and through the mesh, I could easily make out the footsteps leading through the foot-deep snow.

Time to play.

Grinning, I sprinted after her regardless of my swollen length trapped inside my jeans. My arms and legs pumped, my chest ready to fucking explode with excitement. With the goddamn bloodlust that threatened my sanity.

I wanted to bathe in her tears, her blood. Drink

down her cries. Thrust into her heat and take until oblivion burst through my balls.

Where are you, little princess?

Pine trees rose ahead of me, their branches sagging from wet snow, and I slowed, my exhales loud inside my mask. Footsteps disappeared between the trees, and I stalked onward, swiping gathering white from my mask's eyeholes.

A flash of blue rose ahead between more pines.

She sure as fuck hadn't gotten far, her legs flagging, her body struggling to continue through the deep snow.

I wished for nicer weather. Warmth. A green carpet beneath her feet. A chance for her to really believe she could escape me in the woods. A good hour's worth of cat and mouse where the scent of her fear would lead me right to her.

But in this weather, the cold would kill her before her break from reality drew to a close.

Time to end her hope.

Letting out a growl, I barreled toward the stumbling woman ahead of me.

"No!" she shrieked and weaved left, but she didn't stand a chance.

I slammed into her back, and we fell forward, an oomph ripping from lips even though I managed to keep some of my weight off her. Face down in the snow, she struggled beneath me, flailing with useless determination as I grasped her hands over her head.

She'd lost weight, but her ass…

Goddamn.

I pushed more of my mass onto her backside.

She stilled.

And I ground against her, letting her know how her running affected me, how much I wanted to shove my dick into her puckered hole. Make her cry. Make her bleed.

"Get off me you sick fuck!" Her voice was muffled by the snow I still held her in.

Oh, I'd *get off*, alright. Grinning, I soaked in the rush of adrenaline, the lust rippling over my heated skin.

I held her wrists in one hand and slid the other down along her body, groping a breast on my way southward and ignoring the sting of snow against the back of my hand. She still had lush tits, her pebbled nipples hard and cold beneath the thin fabric.

Fuck.

Tiny waist, way too fucking small.

The swell of her hip in my hand—I fucking lifted her tight against my groin, letting a groan escape me as my heart raced as fast as the flying snowflakes.

She attempted to dislodge me, but I wouldn't be moved. "Get off!" she screamed again.

I am.

Eyes closed, lost to lust, lost to fucking humanity, I grunted, thrusting against her ass, my balls brewing with the need to explode. Like a goddamn animal, I was ready to have what I'd been wanting forever. I imagined trapping her beneath me. Ripping into her body. Taking what I'd dreamed about.

"Jackass," she hissed.

My eyelids popped open as the nickname took me back to the first day we'd met and I'd called her a princess.

Frigid as fuck wind whipped at the shirt on my back. Cold ice bit into my hand still gripping her hip. The howl of the storm promised to do us in if we lingered much longer.

Fuck.

I hopped up, pulling Addilyn along up into my arms and trapping her against my chest where she shivered.

She attempted to wiggle, but I crushed her body tight to mine, turned, and headed back to the cabin with quick, sure steps.

To warmth. Safety from hypothermia.

She'd won a round by bringing me back from my bloodlust, but we had all the time in the world.

We could play another day.

13

Addilyn

I was nothing more than a fly stuck in his web. Powerless to fight against his superior strength.

Teeth chattering, head pounding, I gave in to the truth and let my captor carry me back the way I'd fled.

Nothing lay around us but cold, snow-covered wilderness. I blinked against the white swirling in my face. No distant lights. Just wind and biting bits of snow stinging my neck and bare legs.

Heat radiated from his chest, but I refused to rest my cheek against him no matter how much my body wished to melt and soak in the life-sustaining heat.

He smelled like woodsmoke, and he felt like pure, rock-hard muscle.

I shivered, whimpering and telling myself it was due to the cold, not from how he'd held me down.

Restrained my hands. Touched me when I'd told him not to. Thrust his hardness against my ass.

My core pulsed, and I scowled, hating how arousal flooded through me amidst the snowstorm and probably the beginnings of hypothermia.

I hadn't ever gotten the chance to run from Lloyd, hadn't ever been chased, and I wondered briefly if doing so would have turned me on too.

Run, my captor had said in my ear, and even though his unexpected closeness had made me shriek with surprise, lust had slipped in alongside the adrenaline rush over possible escape.

What the hell is wrong with me?

He pushed open the small cabin's door, and warmth swept over us. A grunt and kick behind him shut us inside.

Silence descended except for the crackle of the fire and our heavy breaths.

Still, he clung to me, not putting me on my feet or allowing me a chance to run again.

Not that I would in that damn weather.

There was no place to go.

No hope.

My chest hollowed out, and I swallowed hard as shivers wracked through me. My teeth clattered together.

He grabbed a large bowl while crossing the kitchen area and tossed me into the bedroom, the metal piece clanging at my feet before I collapsed beside it in weakness.

The light tripped off, leaving me in darkness.

Alone.

Still cold as hell and shivering in my wet shirt.

I managed to crawl to the bed, curling up into a ball and burying myself beneath the lone blanket.

Without strength. Hopeless.

Tears slid down my cheeks, wetting the mattress beneath me, and I didn't bother wiping them away. Hollowness swelled inside my chest.

I slept and woke warmer, my T-shirt dry.

Starved.

Darkness still coated the bedroom, and I shifted to sit on the mattress's edge. The scent of something savory filled my nose.

Stomach growling, I pushed up to stand and felt my way around the room to the chair.

A new tray.

I downed the bowl of tepid stew.

Once finished, I crept toward the door. No noise rose from beyond, but I banged against it anyway.

"I have to pee!"

Nothing.

I repeated myself a half-dozen times, letting out curses as the minutes slowly ticked by.

He'd left me in the dark—and I located the metal bowl he'd tossed into the room with me. Having no choice, I settled it into the corner farthest from the bed and relieved myself in the old-fashioned bedpan.

At least the asshole gave me napkins with the stew so I had something to wipe myself.

I shuffled back to the bed. Curled up. Gave into despondency, into the hopelessness settling into my brain and on my shoulders.

***

Minutes, hours passed.

Six meals came and went between bouts of lucidity. Two longer durations of sleep.

Two days of darkness with nothing but my increasingly depressing thoughts to keep me company. I scraped all the dried cum from my torso. Ran my fingers through my ratty hair, thankful for its shorter length. I used one of the cups of water he left me to at least dribble over the apex of my thighs into the chamber pot.

Every time I woke, I knew he'd been in the room. Fresh water and fresh food awaited me. He emptied my bedpan.

He definitely had night vision on that camera up in the corner, I didn't doubt.

I sat and rocked on the bed, rubbing my arms. I'd gotten used to staring into darkness, counting until I lost track of the numbers. Sang every song I could remember. Recited every fable and fairy tale from my childhood still alive in my brain.

I relived my favorite movies from start to finish, taking care not to rush the action of each scene. Even Stolen, my old favorite stalker Stockholm Syndrome movie Jenny and I had loved back in high school.

Not so alluring or hot now that I experienced that shit firsthand.

I paced from wall to wall, avoiding my bedpan whenever it needed emptying.

But I refused to break down and bang on the door or beg and plead. My captor was beneath me—and I wouldn't allow him to feel otherwise.

He never opened the door while I was awake.

Eventually, I lay on the bed, limp and uncaring. My backbone had almost reached its end—but at least he hadn't broken my mind. I found myself wishing Lloyd would show up so the monotony would stop eating away at my brain. Hollowness deepened in my chest like I'd never known, accompanied by a slower pulse, shallower breathing.

All traces of fear dissipated as familiar depression stole my desire to live.

But this time, I didn't have Ciarra to pull me from the depths.

I had no one.

14

Gideon

Three full days of solitary confinement like I'd had my first week in jail—but in the dark like she fucking deserved—and Addilyn refused to give in to panic and tears. Refused to break down in an emotional rage.

Where the fuck she'd gotten her strength from, I had no clue. She'd always been a snobby, spoiled brat, so her quietness surprised me. Still, I sat in silence, telling myself I wasn't in awe of her, choosing instead to focus on my rising anger over failing to break her. Watching as she attempted to amuse herself, same as I'd done during the long, lonely hours in jail.

Not once did she break down or scream for me to let her go to feed the need inside me. She didn't even pound on the door demanding to use the bathroom. Instead, she took to the bowl I'd given her as though she knew the real reason I'd tossed it into her cell with her.

The night-vision camera only allowed me green and white video on the old iPad I'd gotten from Twinkie's friend, but I still enjoyed the fuck out of seeing her on its screen. Watching her squat over the bowl to relieve herself. Wipe her pussy dry. Wipe the ass I wanted to wreck. Her mouth moved as though she conversed with herself, holding my attention.

I should have gotten a damn mic along with the camera so I could be entertained by whatever shit she spewed.

She shifted in her sleep, sometimes pulling up a leg and giving me a peek at her pussy.

Twice while sneaking in food, I studied her sprawled form in the light spilling through the open doorway.

Tempted to touch the swell of her tits.

Contemplating shooting my spunk all over her filthy body again.

But my toughness won out, same as hers.

I wouldn't give in to my animal instinct to take. Seeing her break, the tears and pleading, would be worth it.

When not watching her and practicing self-control over wanting to jerk off, I read all the tattered western paperbacks Twinkie's late uncle had left. Fed the fire. Cooked. Enjoyed the fucking silence and the wilderness stretching around us.

The snow stopped, and I trampled out into it sometimes for hours on end to fill my lungs, take in the mountains, and strain my muscles by climbing the hills beyond Twinkie's cabin.

I turned the cell on once a day to check messages. Over a dozen from Lloyd, demanding answers, to know where we were, how long until he could have his time with her.

I only ever answered with one word: **Soon**.

With every day that passed, he grew more irritated, and I reveled in the fact he didn't know where we were, would never find us unless I gave him coordinates or brought him to the cabin myself.

Making him powerless, knowing anxiety and stress battled in his gut, gave me the sweetest sense of satisfaction, but I would have more.

The anticipation of eventually watching the princess lose it to fear rushed through me like an addictive high I expected would surpass the pleasure I took from keeping Lloyd in suspense.

On day four, she woke, stirring but not bothering to right her shirt that had ridden up while she'd slept. Rather than roll from bed and seek out the food I'd left like she usually did, she stayed put.

Blinked in the darkness while I watched in green and white.

She stared, unmoving.

Minutes ticked by. A fucking hour. Still, she didn't move.

She'd fucking broken, I realized with a scowl, but not how I'd planned or wanted.

She hadn't gone down sobbing. I hadn't managed to make her feel less-than. Sure, she'd flipped when I'd held her down in the snow, but her instinctive need to survive hadn't taken over. Addilyn hadn't lost her poise or her fucking spine in the way I craved.

She'd merely fucking caved to despondency.

After two more hours, I knew she wouldn't eat, the stubborn bitch. I couldn't allow her to waste away. Too many weeks lay between her and her twenty-first birthday.

She needed to live so Lloyd would lose out on all he'd been working toward since marrying her cunt of a mother.

Cursing, I pulled on the damn mask, strode toward the door, and all but busted it down, flicking on the light.

She didn't rouse, merely shutting her eyes against the brightness.

"Get up," I barked.

The snobby princess didn't so much as twitch, as though she couldn't be bothered with my voice and commands.

I yanked her to her feet, thankful as fuck for the gas mask since she hadn't washed for days and probably stank like shit. She sagged in my arms, boneless.

What would get her sputtering and acting like a

living being rather than a corpse? The hissing wildcat I enjoyed the hell out of and missed? A good hard fuck, but that wasn't on the menu yet.

Frigid as fuck water from the showerhead would do. I tossed her into the stall, shirt and all, where she sank to her knees.

She shivered and shook, eyeing my boots. I backed off, leaving the shower curtain open as the cold water beat down on her head.

"Wash," I barked and planted myself in the doorway, legs spread and arms crossed.

The water eventually warmed, steam rising, and she let out one final shiver before standing and tugging off her old shirt, dropping it with a splat to the shower floor.

In an attempt to ignore her pale skin and the lush curve of her ass, I thought on the plans still before me, the ruination of Sheriff Bradshaw thanks to Rogers's files.

A shit ton of shady dealings had taken place between Devon's dad and Rogers. Evidence acquired at three drug busts—evidence that never made it to the station but got re-routed and sold elsewhere. The money was pocketed by Sheriff Bradshaw and Rogers, a shady ex-cop.

He'd promised me pictures, good ones clearly depicting the fucker trading cash for stolen guns and confiscated drugs.

Rogers had been planning to set him up for

months, but the sheriff had gotten wind of his actions and had him locked up before he'd been able to unleash hell.

Being a smart fucker, Rogers had created files on an old USB stick and hid it at his nephew's house. One I hadn't gotten a chance to sniff out before nabbing my prize.

Addilyn Jane Reed.

She was rosy-skinned from the hot water cascading down over her body. Suds covered her head but not the peach-scented kind I'd have preferred. A deodorant soap bar swept over her body, cleaning away days' worth of stink and grime.

She kept her back to me, retaining some bit of privacy, but little did she know, her ass turned me on just as much as her front.

My dick swelled inside my jeans, but I ignored the discomfort.

The bar of soap slipped from her hand and fell to the floor beside the soaked shirt that tickled my memory.

She fucking bent over to retrieve the soap, legs straight, ass cheeks separating and giving me a glimpse of her puckered hole, ridding the thoughts of her shirt from my mind.

"Fuck," I swore under my breath, my dick twitching. Instantly pre-cum welled at the tip.

She washed between her legs—fucking slid soapy

fingers down that crack. Slick. Hot. Probably tight as fuck.

I imagined her asshole sucking my dick into her body, her whimpers from the stretching pain, her tears…

If I didn't jerk off, I'd end up fucking her like a goddamn animal.

Couldn't have that.

With a flick of the button, I quickly unzipped and slid my palm over my leaking head and down until my jeans stopped the motion.

She stepped sideways beneath the spray to rinse, keeping that ass all up in my face, and I palmed my slickened head, squeezing, sliding a few inches to my jeans and back up.

Fucking over and around, my hips thrusting.

"Goddamnit," I hissed as the blue shirt's origins flashed through my head.

Mine. From five years earlier when I'd pressed her against her bedroom door, letting her feel the hardness of my dick for the first time. I'd emptied my balls minutes later in my bedroom, using that shirt to wipe off my cum-soaked hand.

"Fuck."

Addilyn stilled.

I cursed again as my balls exploded. She'd been wearing it to bed every night—my goddamn shirt. Cum shot into my palm, and I shuddered, hips thrusting, spunk erupting.

I finished, but she didn't move. My breath sounded hollow in the mask, and I cursed at myself for the sense of possessiveness that had sent me over the edge.

What did it matter if I took from her physically? What part of me refused to plunder her before she broke so I could laugh in her face? Why did a shred of decency reside deep inside me over a woman who deserved my anger, the revenge I'd promised myself?

The goddamn blue shirt...I still fucking cared, same as her.

Jaw tight, I flicked on the water in the sink and washed the proof of my weakness from my palm.

She made me feeble, that stubborn connection between us keeping me from taking what I'd dreamed about.

Fucking bitch.

I tucked my dick away, yanked a towel from beneath the sink, and shortened the distance between us. "Get out." Shutting off the water, I shoved the towel against her back, and she turned enough to grasp at it, to keep it from falling to the shower floor beside *my* soaked shirt.

Spinning, I strode out the door and into the living area of the cabin where I'd dragged the bureau. I grabbed a clean T-shirt from the top drawer and stomped back the way I'd come, slinging it at her where she stood in the middle of the bathroom.

It fell at her feet.

I stood and stared, forming fists at my sides so I wouldn't grab her, waiting for her to obey.

Her gaze dropped down over me, lingering on my right hand clenched tight by my thigh. I stretched out my fingers beneath her gaze, my body buzzing with need—to punch something, someone. Fucking figured, since I knew I could never truly hurt Addilyn.

She eyed the shirt I'd tossed her way a second before squatting to pick it up.

Black, long-sleeved like the one I wore.

With her focus on my mask, she dropped the damn towel like she wanted to tempt the lusting animal inside me but shrugged the shirt over her wet head before my instincts pushed me to make a move.

Fucking tease—even if her eyes didn't state as much. She'd used the bathroom in front of me without hesitation. Lifted her shirt to sit on the toilet, uncaring that I stood in front of her, feet separating me from her pussy. Yes, she'd kept her back to me in the shower, but maybe she somehow knew her backside made me hard.

Bitch.

A muscle ticked in my jaw, and I once more grabbed her arm, ready to toss her ass back into the bedroom, away from me and my lust.

Addilyn

I'd already been through hell, and there was nothing my captor could do to hurt me. That truth had led to finding peace during the days of darkness he'd kept me in. I refused to call it anything else. Waiting for Lloyd continued to twist my mind, my stomach.

I couldn't look at the damn mask of the man who'd stood before me, but his fisted hands reminded me so much of Gideon that my eyes stung, revealing my weakness. The shirt I pulled down over my head to cover my nakedness hinted at the scent of his skin I'd sniffed from the old blue shirt left behind in a soaked pile on the shower floor.

Wishful thinking.

The energy crackled between us, raising the hairs on my neck, and I told myself it wasn't Gideon, to not get my hopes up. The man in front of me was too large, his shoulders too wide, his neck too thick.

But the bulge in his jeans reminded me of the hard length Gideon had slid between my lips. Five years later, and I still remembered the saltiness of his cum, the lust in his eyes as he'd peered down at me with his hooded gaze. His lips had parted as he'd thrust, fucking my throat until I'd gagged.

My captor had jerked off while I showered—I knew, I could feel the tension thick in the air between us—but I hadn't turned to look. Couldn't. I'd frozen in fear over what he might do if he caught sight of my pebbled nipples and the thrum of my heartbeat in my neck as the hot water had trailed over my body, rinsing soap and shampoo down the drain.

Once more, he grabbed hold of my arm, but I didn't stumble after him as he crossed the living area.

I expected to be tossed and locked in the dark bedroom, but he pulled a sheet from the bottom drawer of a dresser in the kitchen area and slapped it against my chest.

"Strip the bed," he stated. His hollow, low tone was short and gruff as though I'd offended him.

Happy to do as told, I set to work, ridding my bed of the dirty sheet and fitting the new one atop the mattress. When I finished, I turned to face him, hands clasped in front of me and chin lifting as if to say, "Go ahead. Lock me back up."

I wanted him to see that the shower had revived me from the near-stupor I'd chosen to call peace, the consideration for my state once more rousing that seed of hope in my breast to sprout. The arousal tingling between my thighs over memories of Gideon reminded me I still lived.

But my stomach rumbled.

"I'm hungry," I said, lifting my chin even higher, steadily eyeing his mask with disdain even though it freaked me the fuck out and made my feet itch to run.

"You can eat the eggs I left you earlier this morning."

I glanced at the tray sitting on the lone chair. "They're cold."

He stalked toward me, and I stepped deeper into the bedroom until the mattress bumped the backs of my legs. The upward swing of his hand made me flinch, but he grasped my neck rather than hitting me. Hardened fingers dug into my flesh, and I stilled, my pulse thrumming beneath his hold.

Breath heavy, he leaned down into my face, close enough I wanted to turn my eyes away from the mask—but refused.

"Want me to heat them up?" he whispered harshly. "Make you a new mug of tea? Get you a fresh cup of water?"

Spine stiffening as much as possible, I went for confident even while my insides quaked. "I would appreciate it, yes."

"I'm not your fucking maid, princess. Eat the goddamn food or starve." He squeezed my neck and pushed off me, spinning on his heel and slamming the door on his way out.

I found my balance, blinking, his words processing…

Princess.

Gideon. It's him…it's really him.

My breath left in a rush along with the strength in my legs, and I sank onto the bed, my insides alight with fire even as shivers wracked through me.

I swallowed hard as I envisioned the boy I'd known turning into the man who'd been watching me for weeks. Those wide shoulders, the muscle mass he'd put on… Would the face behind the mask be the same? That glint in his eyes the one that haunted my dreams?

Gideon Destil had five more years left to his sentence yet somehow had found freedom.

How? And why hadn't I heard?

And he'd kidnapped me. Hated me for my betrayal—but he didn't intend to kill me. He also had no intention of touching me…

My eyes stung, and my hands clenched on my lap so I wouldn't chew on my fingernails. Even though my heart raced, my throat tightened.

Gideon.

Mere feet away, but his heart and mind were miles further because of my betrayal. Guilt filled me with self-loathing, same as it had ever since I'd stood witness in court.

Had he taken me captive for Lloyd? Was he getting back at me for what I'd done? If the first was true, why hadn't his father shown up? It'd been what…four? Five days since he'd taken me? A full week?

I'd lost track of time.

The storm had abated, I'd noted while being dragged to the bathroom, but wilderness stretched through both of the small cabin's windows, a dim winter's afternoon.

Definitely not in Anchorage, and definitely not a landscape I'd recognized in the snowstorm while attempting to escape.

We could be anywhere in Alaska.

And he could be holding me captive and waiting for anything…anyone.

Why?

I stared at the door he'd slammed, sure and yet disbelieving Gideon stood beyond it. Perhaps he sat on the couch, his brain just as busy, his emotions in as much turmoil as mine.

Five years had created the types of changes in his body I wouldn't have recognized if it weren't for the way he fisted his hands and the hated pet name he'd called me. While I doubted prison had been kind on his mind, he'd certainly taken care of his body.

I considered how he'd striped my torso with his cum when I laid tied to the bed, how he'd jerked off while I'd showered, and arousal flooded through me. With my hands clasped on my lap, I chewed on my lower lip. Glancing up into the room's corner, I wondered if he watched through the camera. What went through his mind. How he felt.

What would he do if I dragged the chair over, climbed up, and ripped the damn thing off the wall?

Would he come in? Rage at me? Give me a chance to talk to him?

My stomach churned over not knowing. Kidnapping me was a crime punishable by more jail time. Lloyd had told me Gideon hated me—but what if Lloyd had lied? What if Gideon believed I despised him? That I'd intentionally gone along with the prosecution to get him the full ten-year sentence?

I wouldn't put it past Lloyd to tell him one thing and me another.

Hadn't that monster hidden the truth from Mother for years? Declared his undying love, his inability to even look at another woman due to her breath-stealing beauty? A liar of the worst sort, he'd whispered the same to me upon sneaking into my room once Mother passed out with her sleeping pills or alcohol.

Lloyd lied.

And Gideon and I had both suffered because of it.

But could I convince him of that truth?

I'd never given him any indication I appreciated his protection. I'd never been anything but a snobby bitch, looking down my nose at him as though he'd been less than, when in reality, he'd been more than I could have possibly known I'd wanted.

Needed.

Tears stung my eyes, and I laid on my side, focus still on the door.

The next time he came in, I would gauge his anger by the set of his shoulders and the hands at his sides. Knowing my captor was Gideon made the rest easier.

I closed my eyes, not feeling so alone after all.

16

Gideon

Like an idiot, I fucked up and called her princess. She'd heard me and caught on to the truth of my identity if how she loosened and settled in with no trace of fear was any indication.

Knowing who I was, she had to expect I wanted revenge for her part in getting me put away.

So why relax?

The question haunted me for hours while I carried in firewood from the tarped stack outside nearly covered in snow. Bitter wind bit at my exposed face, but at least the white shit had stopped flying.

We were snowed in big time. I peered down the dirt road leading from civilization to Twinkie's cabin. Thank fuck I had enough provisions to see us through for a few weeks.

At least we weren't so far off the fucking path I didn't have cell service.

It was time to rethink my plan.

I stomped my boots free of snow and kicked them off to sit by the fire. Perched on the couch's edge, I powered on my cell, thoroughly expecting a shit ton of texts from Lloyd.

He didn't disappoint, the final at about fifty with one sent not ten minutes earlier.

Where are you?

With Addilyn, I texted back.

The phone rang, but I didn't pick up.

Lloyd: **Answer the goddamn phone.**

Me: **No.**

Lloyd: **You've had your time with her. Tell me where you are so I can finish this.**

Me: **She hasn't broken yet.**

Lloyd: **Then up your game. Time is dwindling. If it's money you want, let me know how much. It's yours.**

I snorted. The days drew short for him. I had all I wanted and then some. As for the cash, I didn't need a goddamn thing from him except revenge. **I'll be in touch.**

I turned off my cell and sat in silence, eyeing the rich snob on the camera who'd shown her pretentious nature enough that I'd messed up.

Her sass and her demands didn't turn me on like they'd used to—she'd pissed me the fuck off, and I'd lost the tight control I held over my emotions. Seeing that glimpse of the old Addilyn, the one I'd lusted for...

Fuck. I scrubbed a hand over my face, scratching at the few days' worth of scruff along my jawline.

So, what to do?

I'd planned to wreck her, but with how peaceful she seemed after finding out her captor was her sick stepbrother... Like she didn't hate or fear me. Like she could rest even knowing her circumstances as my captive. Like she believed I had zero intentions of hurting her.

"Fuck."

The tangle of emotions, the push/pull that had always existed between us made me antsy. I got up and heated up a large can of beef stew, all the while going back to the iPad to watch her sleep.

Like a goddamn baby.

I hadn't terrorized her nearly enough. Hadn't come close to breaking her. Her resolve, her strength hadn't diminished except for making her lethargic upon waking.

The shower had given her new life.

Time for me to steal it away.

Mask in place, I walked into her room, and she sat, blinking. Ignoring her, I retrieved her breakfast tray and stalked back out, slamming and locking the door before she could breathe a word.

No dinner.

No extra water or tea.

Not a goddamn thing.

My way of letting the little princess know she'd eat what she was offered and when—or she could fucking starve. The rich, spoiled bitch deserved to go without for a change, same as I'd done for five long as fuck years.

Flicking off her light from outside of the room, I expected a grin to stretch my lips. So why the fuck did my stomach twist? Why did I scowl when I once more found her lying down—and fucking smiling?

"The fuck?" I yanked the old camera screen closer to my face, staring at the live feed.

A soft upward curve of her lips suggested pleasure.

My brain buzzed as I tried to figure her out.

Lloyd had told me she hated me and had planned along with her mother to have me tossed into the slammer for statutory rape. It'd been her testimony that got me locked up for five years...so what the fuck?

She seemed relaxed, same as before she'd fallen asleep, like she felt fucking safe or some shit.

How was that possible? The fuck...

Lloyd lied.

Jaw clenching, I considered the thought, my disgust over my father growing with every second. He'd wanted her—I didn't fucking doubt that truth. Those old, supposedly covered records of mine mysteriously showing up in the prosecutor's hands suggested he had needed me gone. For good. Where I couldn't fuck with whatever plans he had for his stepdaughter.

If what I speculated was truth, *had* Lloyd gotten his hands on her? I considered how she'd done a one-eighty from the vibrant wildcat in high school and the depression and lack of...life she'd exhibited while I'd stalked her the previous couple of weeks.

Scrubbing a hand over my face, I whispered a few more curses, my goddamn brain fucked the hell up as pieces of the puzzle in my mind tried to click together.

I hated her.

I wanted to hurt her in every way imaginable.

I lusted for her body and the energy between us that always made me so goddamn hard as a teen that I'd jacked off countless times a day.

Calculating and observant were two traits I'd always prided myself in...how the fuck had I missed the truth? *Was* it the truth? Or was there another puzzle piece I hadn't yet been aware of?

Torn and unsure—fucking hating not being in control—I banked the fire and curled up on the uncomfortable couch.

Maybe the morning would bring some clarity before my goddamn restraint snapped.

I woke hard as a fucking rock. Lust simmering in my balls.

The camera showed she sat all prim and proper on the edge of the bed. Hands lightly clasped on her lap. Facing the door in the dark.

Waiting for me.

Cool and composed when all I fucking wanted was for her to lose her shit and become *less than.*

I tossed the camera aside and stood in front of her door, hands fisted. Balls throbbing and my head a fucking mess.

I'd dreamed of the night she'd sucked me down like a goddamn queen. Peered up at me with those eyes…innocent and full of need I swore to fucking God I hadn't imagined.

But I'd seen fear that night too.

I hadn't been able to break her by keeping her in the darkness, even though the nightlight beside her bed back home had suggested she hated it. Hadn't brought on tears by forcing the princess to piss in a bowl. Couldn't even rouse shame to redden her face when standing in front of her while she'd used the toilet and showered.

Breathing deep, I closed my eyes, allowing the thoughts of exactly how I could knock Addilyn Reed down a few pegs.

Take her like the instincts in me demanded. Like my dick ached for.

Regardless of what truth led us to where we both

waited for the clash between us, I would have what I'd been dreaming about for over five years.

Couldn't move forward without it.

No fucking mask stretched over my head—because what would be the point? I would show her the man I was deep inside, the one without restraint, the sick fuck who dreamed of laying waste to her body, her mind.

I would have what I lusted for without asking for it.

Make her cry.

Break the princess I had wanted since the day I first laid eyes on her.

Pushing against my humanity, the part of me that always roused my protective nature toward her, I shoved into her door, my rage and need ruling.

Flicked on the light.

She blinked twice, but no shock widened her eyes as they focused on me in the bedroom doorway. I gave her a few seconds of freedom, gave her enough to hope for release, for an escape in her future.

And she took those few seconds to look over my six-foot-three inches, the extra pounds I'd added on, the shorter hair atop my head, and the dark scruff along my jaw.

Our gazes finally collided—and fucking held as that connection I remembered between us once more rose to choking levels. Fucking stole my breath. Ripped every idea for revenge from my goddamn head.

Calmed my inner anger…

So much for that fucking plan of taking her pussy in order to break her.

I stared. Unable to think, unable to move. Caught up in her eyes, clear and seeing. Accepting. That draw deep inside, like our souls entwined was same as it had been all those years ago—as though no fucking time had passed.

Without a word, she stood. Licked her goddamn lower lip and approached me on whisper-quiet feet, every step causing a shot of adrenaline to pulse through my blood while I stood frozen.

Unfucking hinged.

Big blue eyes unafraid, without a hint of her usual snobbery, peered up at me. Held me ensnared.

She laid her palm against my chest. So tiny and yet so warm…the touch melted clear to my cold heart.

A shudder ripped through me, tempting me to *like* her again.

"Don't touch me," I stated through clenched teeth, hands fisted at my sides.

"You won't hurt me," she whispered, glancing down at her fingertips that had to feel the pounding of my heart beneath my shirt.

"I could," I tossed out with a sneer.

"But you won't. I know you." Those blue eyes

once more lifted, pupils dilating as though she wanted to fucking pick up right where we'd left off five years ago.

Her, a supposed grieving girl, while I'd been hauled off in cuffs, powerless to stay with her and protect her, like every inch of my body had longed to do.

But not anymore.

My blood pumped harder at the memories of her whispering the word that had sealed my fate. How she'd refused to look at me while walking out of the courtroom, her chin lifted like the haughty bitch she was. Roused back to life, my anger clenched my jaw once more.

The princess thought she knew me…she had no fucking clue the man I'd become after her betrayal and my stint in jail. An aggressive predator in sheep's clothing.

Stupid, stupid girl.

I *could* wreck her.

I would.

The drive for revenge over the previous five years demanded it.

My hand found her neck, and she grabbed at my wrist, her lips parting on a gasp.

My adrenaline and lust spiked at the fear filling her eyes, and I stalked forward, pushing her backward until she slammed against the wall.

17

Addilyn

My nerve endings sparked to life like a burst of fireworks, igniting raging need inside me. Arousal swelled between my thighs, hot and heavy, causing my nipples to pebble and my heart to pound.

His grasp on my neck scared the shit out of me, but holy fucking hell...

I should have fought his hold or demanded he let me go. Instead, my body relaxed against the wall, warm and wet, begging for more. My grip on his wrist loosened in submission to his control, but I kept my hand on him, needing the skin-on-skin connection. We shared heavy breaths inches apart as I stared into ice-like eyes swarming with an intensity I didn't recognize.

The anger, the tension radiating off him heated me to the point my skin prickled with awareness.

Hairs raised on my nape, my arms, but I didn't heed the instinctive nudge to fight or flee.

I melted like a desperate whore.

His fingers tightened, cutting off my oxygen—and I let him. Longed for it. Trembled for it.

I wished he'd choke me out, that he'd wake me by shooting cum all over my body. But more than that, I desired *him* and all he'd promised me five years earlier.

Gasping for air, hovering on passing out, I released his wrist and once more touched his heaving chest, his hard muscle hot even through the cotton T-shirt. What could I do but tell him the truth after so many lies? He deserved it for all I'd done, deserved to have me prove him right about how I would one day beg him to touch me.

I licked my lip and held his gaze. "Fuck me, Gideon," I whispered with what air I had left.

His gaze held steady at my choked words, but his grip on my throat eased up, allowing the pinpricks of stars growing in my periphery to fade away. "No."

Our shared breaths came in pants, the energy between us intensifying to the point my skin felt ready to burst into flame. I squeezed my thighs together, completely baffled as to why he would deny what had flared to life the second we'd first seen one another all those years ago.

"Why not?" I sounded like a whiny child even though the words ripped from my lungs.

"Because you *want* it," he muttered harshly through clenched teeth, bringing his face closer to mine.

Because I damn near dripped for his dick—when once upon a time I'd denied him again and again.

Realization dawned as our gazes held.

He didn't crave the Addilyn ready to beg for his dick but the snobby princess he used to know, the one he could manipulate to get on her knees to suck him off. But that girl had gotten squashed deep down inside my soul. Her fire had died out.

All I had left was the kind of fight brought on by the fear of being used. If feigning I didn't crave his touch gained me what my body lusted for...

"So, if I didn't want your dick, you'd take my pussy like the jackass you are," I tried to state firmly while lifting my chin and straightening my shoulders, so damn ready to give him exactly what he'd been after since we were teenagers.

An animalistic gleam lit his eyes, causing my core to clench as he once more tightened his grip on my neck, tipping my head back. "Damn right, princess." He flashed his dimples, and my belly dipped in a swoon, but I didn't give him a chance to respond as a rush of adrenaline coursed through me.

I jerked my knee up—and he shied away with a chuckle.

Fucker.

He wanted a hissing cat? I would lash at him with

every ounce of strength I had left in me if it meant I could finally have him.

Sick or not, given the chance to have what I hadn't admitted to myself I desired as a young girl, I went all in. Desperate for all he'd promised.

For *him.*

I wrenched against his hold and dug my fingernails into his forearm. Kicked and squirmed, fighting to rid myself of his firm hold that continued to make my core throb to be filled.

"Fucking let me go!" I clawed like one pissed off feline, not meaning one damn word of the demands spewing from my lips. Releasing his relentless arm, I swung at his face.

Caught his cheek with my fingernails, dragging to mar his perfection with blood-welling stripes.

"Goddamnit!" His lips thinned as he slammed me against the wall again, his eyes going dark. Hard.

Yes.

Arousal slickened between my thighs, but I kicked—he sidestepped.

"You fucking prick!" I swiped at his face. He whipped his head back away from my reach with another chuckle. "Fucker...let me go!"

Heat, absolute pure adrenaline, and disturbing desire fueled my limbs, and I kicked and swung, soaking in every grunt I earned from his luscious-looking lips. The thump of my fist on his shoulder and my foot to his thigh heightened my core's craving for his dick.

Gideon got smart and held me at arm's length where I couldn't reach him, lifting me higher. Grinning, his eyes filled with lust.

I stood on my tiptoes, my head tipped back against the log wall and his grip tight enough around my throat that darkness started to grow in my periphery. Gasping for oxygen, I flailed with too-short arms and legs.

Need...breath...

"F-fuck you," I whispered and settled on jabbing my fingernails into his forearm again.

He relented the slightest bit as I hovered on the edge of passing out rather than going over. His hooded gaze latched onto my eyes, and he pulled out his dick with his free hand.

I drew blood beneath my fingernails, but he ignored the pain I inflicted, the sound of his zipper causing my pussy to pulse.

"You want my dick, princess?"

"No!" I spat at him, my vision wavering as I struggled to shift my gaze lower, to watch his hand smear pre-cum all over his hard length.

Oh God...

My mouth watered.

My core clenched over the schlicking noise of fist fucking.

And I dug my fingernails deeper into his arm. He

didn't flinch but lifted me by my goddamn throat like I was insubstantial. A toy for him to play with, to toss around.

I attempted a weakened kick, and he stepped in between my legs. The back of his hand holding his dick brushed against my soaked pussy with every stroke down his length.

The sounds of his hand moving between our wetness made my heartbeat thrum, and his knuckles rubbing over my clit rushed tingles up through my quivering legs that widened involuntarily. I craved him—needed him inside me, giving us what we both lusted for.

"Let me go," I croaked out, attempting to be what he wanted up to the edge of the cliff we approached.

His hold on my neck lessened as he bent his knees to touch the head of his dick against my pussy. He paused from taking me, his gaze narrowing and his lips parting on a quick inhale. "Never."

He thrust his entire length into me with one deep grunt—and the world stopped at my gasp of unrestricted oxygen over the violent intrusion.

Gazes collided, ensnared.

Hearts pounding as we existed in timeless space. Together…as one.

My ears rang, and my full lungs seized at the sting of his girth, of him finally…*finally* having me.

"Gideon…" My breath rushed out on a sob of pent-up longing. Relief. Pain at the harsh claiming.

A tear slid down my cheek, and his dick jerked inside me.

"Fuck yes." He leaned in to lick the droplet, his tongue like silk on my skin, his slick, calloused hand lifting my thigh higher to his hip.

I allowed him that one second of satisfaction while cinching my legs around his waist to keep him where I wanted him, regardless of the stinging stretch my body fought to accommodate. My hands found his shorter hair as his thickness throbbed inside me. Unmoving, as though he savored the clasp of my pussy straining around his entire length.

His hand slid from my waist to grasp my ass, his mouth running along my jawline toward mine—and I bit his lower lip.

He took my mouth and fucked into me so damn hard I gasped in his exhaled sweet breath…so damn delicious. Fireworks and racing shivers swept over me with every lash of his tongue and each thrust of his hips that banged my back against the wall, without a doubt marking my skin.

Utter, maddening perfection. Pain and pleasure. Everything I had ever dreamed of.

But I didn't relax into the violence between us that only made me wetter. I gave him the fight he wanted.

"Fucking hate you," I lied, pulled at his hair and scraping my teeth over his hungry mouth as his hip bones slammed into me, his fingers digging into my ass cheek to keep me from escaping.

I bucked against him, meeting his every grunted thrust. We both cursed. Bit and grasped at flesh in our need to be closer. The sting between my thighs didn't relent, and the bruising of my back against the logs added to my sick arousal smearing between our groins.

He took.

And so did I.

All that had been denied us, fulfilling the lust that hadn't diminished in our time apart.

18

Gideon

She cursed at me—fucking cried—while I attempted to break her body against the cabin's wall. Hisses and moans…biting nails and sharp teeth drawing blood and making me rage, feeding the animal inside me.

My princess with a goddamn backbone of steel.

I couldn't remember a pussy as hot and tight as hers. Couldn't remember any other girl I'd fucked.

Addilyn was my body and mind's sole focus. Her clutching heat around my throbbing dick with every deep-seated thrust the only thing I could think about. The wetness of her smearing all over my pelvis created one hell of a fucking mess.

Gasps and moans turned me light-headed as fuck, rushed tingles through my chest. Curses and the schlicking sound of dirty fucking, the slapping of skin, were my deepest fantasies come to life.

And the scent of our combined arousal, the musk of her desire, flooded my nose and made me impatient to own her in every way possible.

My balls drew up tight, and I pulled away from her intoxicating mouth. Needed to see her face. Watch her as I brought her release.

Hazed and bright blue, still wet with tears, her eyes latched onto mine, same as they'd done five years ago while she'd gagged on my dick.

I grasped her ass, digging my fingers in hard enough that she whimpered past swollen, reddened lips I wanted to devour all over again. A mouth I wouldn't ever grow tired of tasting. Sweet cherries and slick softness.

Maddening, fucking perfection.

My other hand found her neck again, and I held her against the wall, thrusting my length into her over and over. Losing myself in her body.

In her eyes.

She clung to my forearm, panting.

"I want you to come," I grunted, shoving deeper into her. Harder. Making her wince with every slam against her womb. "Fucking need to feel you break all over my dick. Soak me with your cum." My jaw clenched to keep from exploding before she did. "Touch your clit, princess," I said, not losing my rhythm with my hips pounding against hers.

She let go of my wrist. Pupils blown wide, she held my stare—and did as told.

"Oh God." Head tilting back, she stopped fighting me and strummed the fuck out of her little nub.

"Yeah." I drove into her, watching her eyes as they lost focus, her mouth falling open as though ready to scream. "Come all over my dick, princess. Give it to me—"

"G-Gideon!"

Fucking hell, her scream… Wetness erupted from her, soaking my dick.

"O-Oh!"

Her pussy clamped down on me like a goddamn vise, and she broke like a dam, curses and shrieks flying from her lips.

"So. Fucking. Sexy." Her cum squirted with every grunted word accompanying my thrusts. "You're dripping off my balls, princess. Fuck."

I took her mouth, swallowing her cries and slamming into her like a goddamn animal. Tingles rose in the base of my spine and raced toward my sack as her soaked pussy pulsed around me.

I tore my mouth off hers to find her neck.

"Christ!" I latched my teeth onto her tender flesh and came with blinding ferocity, an explosion of heat rushing up through my length. Every shot of spunk ripped a grunt from my lungs as my dick jerked inside her.

"Jesus…fuck," I gasped against her skin, panting. Groaning with every spurt that shuddered my body.

Fucking perfect.

Absolute fucking torture of the sweetest kind.

She clung to me, trembling as I came, and I kept her pressed against the wall. My dick belonged inside her body, my mouth on her flesh.

I'd stolen her away, and I wasn't ever letting her go.

"Gideon." She ran her fingers through my hair.

I couldn't catch my goddamn breath. A shudder ripped through me, and I peeled my upper body away from hers, keeping her pinned in place with my hips.

Fresh tears slid over her flushed cheeks, and I swiped at them with my thumbs, grasping her head in my hands. "Did I hurt you?"

"Yes."

"Good," I grunted, trying to bury my softening dick in deeper. Overwhelming exhilaration over getting Addilyn the way I'd always wanted her spread warmth through me.

"I liked it," she whispered, her eyes troubled. "Too much."

My lighthearted feeling went away, and a muscle ticked in my jaw at the conflicted look on her face. "No such fucking thing."

She swallowed hard, and I stepped back, lifting her off me. A flinch furrowed her brow, and I took sick satisfaction in knowing my thick dick had stretched her to the point of pain.

The black T-shirt settled over her hips as she sagged against the wall.

Thick, white spunk slid down the insides of her thighs, the wetness of her cum dripping down to her goddamn ankles and all over the floor.

Hot as fuck.

I cupped her pussy, letting our combined cum coat my palm. Our gazes once more locked, the connection of old entwining us together. A million thoughts and a slew of emotions I couldn't name swirled like a toxic brew inside my brain and chest.

I'd given in. I'd been the one to break while she had stood stoic and strong. I wasn't sure how to feel about that fact, but she *had* broken on my dick, and I'd never known such euphoria.

I swiped two fingers through the mess between her thighs and brought them up between us.

Coated her swollen lips with our cum.

"Lick."

She didn't flick out her tongue but sucked her lower lip fully into her mouth as though to savor us, her gaze never leaving mine.

"How do we taste, princess?"

"Perfect."

Christ, if her rasped whisper didn't hit me like a shot of lust straight to the groin.

"Fuck." I stepped back, eyeing her hot as fuck mouth. "Take off your shirt."

She did as told, revealing all that pale skin I wanted to mark up and bruise with my fingers. A purple hue already tinted her neck where I'd choked her.

I held out my hand, and she gave me the long-sleeved shirt. Sinking to my knees, I wiped her from pussy to feet before cleaning up my dick and tossing the dirty shirt aside.

With my breath finally caught, I stood, studying her while tucking myself away inside the jeans still hanging off my hips. The denim was wet from her gushed cum. Didn't give a shit…made my dick think about going for round two.

We'd made a wild mess of her shorter curls. Pink flushed cheeks wiped free of the tear tracks I'd caused. Wide blue eyes still slightly dilated. Lips red and swollen.

Her curvy body—too damn thin but still fucking gorgeous—was like the best damn gift karma could ever give me.

"You've changed," I grunted the truth of what I saw.

She glanced over the width of my shoulders, the thickness of my chest. "Your body has too, but you're still the same Gideon."

I tilted my head back and scowled down over my

nose at her. "I'm not the young boy you knew five years ago, princess."

She fucking smiled, a real one like she only used to offer Devon—and same as sunshine, light flooded through me, illuminating parts of the darkness I'd long thought consumed me. The sight stole my goddamn breath.

"I'd like to know the new you," she said, her lips slowly relaxing. "The one I mistakenly, and to my constant shame, helped put behind bars."

Shame…

I stared at her—fucking hard as her smile faded, regret filling her eyes.

"I won't ever ask forgiveness because I don't deserve it," she whispered, her hand once more finding my chest and searing me through the cotton between our skin. "You lost five years of your life over my honesty when I should have lied for you. I am sorry, Gideon. Truly. More than you could ever possibly imagine."

My head stayed tipped back, gaze hooded in attempt to keep from putting myself at her mercy again. I'd thought I could break her, but she'd caused fissures deep inside me instead. Uncertain…I floundered for the first fucking time in insecurities I didn't know I had. "Lloyd said you hated me."

"He told me the same about you."

"He's a fucking liar." I practically spat the words,

even though I'd thought I *had* hated her with every cell in my body.

Addilyn's hand fell away from my chest, and she stepped back, wrapping her arms around her nakedness. "You don't know the half of it."

Her bony shoulders hunched while she hugged her tiny frame. Her head turned, gaze flitting away as though ashamed.

A prickle of unease, of foreboding damn near swallowed me whole, settling in to twist my guts. I grasped her chin, forcing her to face me, needing the truth even though I feared it. "Did he touch you?"

Wetness welled to coat her eyes as she peered up at me. Her pain hit me like a stab to the heart, and I knew the truth before she even breathed a single, goddamn word. Tension roused through me, and breathing grew difficult, my heart thumping heavily.

"Yes," she whispered, causing a roar in my ears.

The same fucking answer that had put me behind bars.

Fuck, how I hated that word.

I forced my jaw to loosen. "Without your consent?" My tone came out level, fucking opposite of how I felt—on edge, tilting toward the type of rage that had caused Devon's three-day coma. The loss of humanity that would end in certain rash decisions and reckless bloodshed.

"Yes." A tear slid down her cheek, and I stared as it dripped off her trembling chin.

A knife twisted in my chest. Sliced down my torso, gutting me.

I hadn't been there for her. Couldn't have sheltered her from that piece of shit while in jail.

"How long have you been wearing my shirt to bed, Addilyn?" I asked, having to know if my suspicions were right.

"Since you were taken away from me." Another tear fell. "And when he...started, I thought maybe it could protect me from him."

Goddamn fucking hell... Fuck!

"I wasn't there," I gasped out, my chest constricting even as rage boiled in my veins.

Addilyn laid her tiny hand on my chest as though to soothe the anger rising inside me. "He would have gotten to me one way or another."

"Tell me," I demanded through gritted teeth.

"I-I don't want to relive it, Gideon."

And I didn't want to fucking hear it, but a sick part deep inside me needed every detail. Every last fucking thing he'd said to her while taking what didn't belong to him.

"I'm going to ruin him, so fuel my fire, Addilyn. Make my revenge that much sweeter."

"Gideon..." She choked on my name, tears rolling with abandon.

"Christ, princess." I pulled her into my arms, just like I'd done all those years ago, but more for my sake than hers. Sinking down onto the mattress, I cradled her against my chest, closed my eyes, and fucking soaked in the soft feel of her. She tucked against me like she belonged there, her tears wetting the shirt her hands grasped at, as though afraid I would dissipate into thin air.

I understood her shakiness, her gulped breaths while quieting. Time halted—or perhaps sped past—as we settled into silence, in a cocoon of warmth and heavy limbs.

"Tell me," I whispered against her silky-soft hair.

And she did.

19

Addilyn

I felt no shame being naked and held against Gideon's hard body. My insides still buzzed from the best fuck of my life, from the connection between us that had snapped into place like a puzzle piece.

Perfectly fit.

The fight, the pain, and the release of cum was like nothing I'd ever experienced before. And he'd found the struggle sexy, hadn't pulled away, hadn't been turned off by how his body and the violence between us had made me come.

With my face against his chest, I breathed him in, pushing away the euphoria that hovered near exhaustion to give him what he asked for—steadying myself for the nightmare I would relive.

I inhaled until it hurt.

"It started sixteen days after they locked you up." My stomach churned at the memory, but I stared at Gideon's shoulder so I wouldn't see the flashbacks behind closed eyelids. "He'd had it planned. Said things couldn't have gone better. He sent Mother away."

A shudder rippled over me, and Gideon grasped the back of my head. Held me tight against him, offering comfort like he'd done all those years ago. The steady thump of his heart beneath my ear soothed me, and I listened for a few moments, thankful to hear its steady beat.

Alive.

Here.

"My protector was gone," I whispered, thin and reedy. "And it was all my fault."

"He would have found a way to get rid of me." His deep voice rumbled, sending a shiver down my spine and reminding me of my own words.

"But you planned on taking off after graduation, didn't you?"

"I did—until the night Devon kissed you. I knew then I would never leave you. Never let you go."

A heavy sigh escaped me, my heart fluttering regardless of the story I needed to tell. "Your father hit me in the temple, enough so I couldn't fight him off but not enough to black out. He threatened me in order to keep me quiet, but I wasn't about break for him. I told Mother."

My eyelids slid shut at the memory of the screaming match between us. The red handprint I'd carried on my cheek for three days.

"Twice after that, he drugged me since I refused to give him what he wanted," I whispered, my guts clenching over the memory.

And my body...

Stomach threatening to heave, I blinked my eyes open. Stared hard at the way the rounded muscle of Gideon's shoulder stretched his shirt while I swallowed against the need to vomit.

"He was rough," I finally managed to continue. "Left me bruised and aching. Took what innocence I had left." My voice caught on a choking swallow to rid the bitter tang in my mouth, but I felt compelled to tell Gideon everything like he'd demanded.

My skin crawled, my cheeks hot, but I forced the words out.

"He made me come." My ragged whisper revealed my deepest shame.

Gideon's chest stopped moving at my words, and I became overly aware of my nakedness. My body tensed, ready to pull away.

"Stay," he stated harshly, his arms like a vise.

I shuddered—hard—and clung to him.

"He broke me, Gideon." Tears slid down my face. Dripped off my chin as I sank into him once more, clutching at his shirt. "I-I can't enjoy sex..."

"Unless you feel threatened. Feel pain."

Nausea stirred to life in my stomach, and I nodded, biting my tongue to keep from puking. Sobbing.

"That's not broken, princess." Gideon shifted me in his arms, turning me around to straddle his hips as he rested against the headboard. His eyes glinted in the light as he caught my gaze.

"It *feels* broken inside," I rasped through my tears, turning away, unable to look at his face.

He cradled my jawline in his calloused hands, leaned in, and licked the droplets from my left cheek. Softly kissed my quivering lips. Licked the other side free of tears.

Lifting my head tighter, he forced me to hold my stare, his eyes hard as flint. "You're goddamn perfect."

Warmth curled in my belly, spreading through my chest. I touched a fingertip to his lips, shushing whatever bull he wanted to spew in his postcoital contentment.

The slight freckles that had once sprinkled over his nose and cheekbones had disappeared. Probably from spending so many years indoors, out of the California sun.

I'd done that to him.

Me.

And in doing so, I'd left myself vulnerable to the real wolf in sheep's clothing.

"He groomed me from day one," I stated past the thickness in my throat, feeling a little bit steadier in my emotions. Even though my tears had ended, I needed to unload all the shit I'd endured. Maybe finally telling the whole story to the one I had failed would somehow ease the burden I carried. "I didn't recognize what it was until years later. He weaseled his way into my head. Became my friend. Manipulated me into trusting him, his word, his promises."

Eventually I had stopped fighting, and he called me his lover. Attempted to be gentle. He'd whispered promises of forever in my ear while I lay like a corpse beneath him, my stare fixed on a wall while he sweated and grunted atop or behind me.

Gideon sat in silence, his hands touching my hair, my neck, my arms, always caressing me as I relived the horrors of those days. He wiped away tears that fell with every recounted incident between his father and me.

Lloyd hadn't ever given me the world like he'd claimed. He'd stolen. Taken what hadn't belonged to him. Each and every time—even if he somehow made my body climax around him.

Rage filled Gideon's eyes, and his muscles tensed beneath me, but he still held steady like a rock. Offering comfort.

I fueled his fire like he'd asked me to, not leaving out a single detail of his father's sexual abuse, Mother's continued disbelief, and my depression. How, on the day I'd turned eighteen, I'd hopped in my car and taken off with no friends, no connections outside of those in Mother and Lloyd's circle.

Mother's credit card supplied me with a cheap hotel room for the remainder of the school year since they didn't come looking for me. And my life became my own. I'd ordered takeout when I could stomach eating. Read books from the library—bags of them to pass the time. Mother paid for it all and never reached out to me for reimbursement.

"Lloyd said she's dead. Overdosed." Gideon's voice held no trace of pity or remorse, and I wasn't surprised we shared the sentiment.

But would he agree with my thoughts over what I believed truly happened?

"She was a drinker, not a pill popper," I said, closing my eyes and waiting, his heart a comforting thump beneath my ear.

"You think Lloyd's responsible?" he asked, his tone guarded, even though his arms hadn't tensed around me.

"I just know my mother, and she never would've taken her own life over fear of what her peers would say."

He grunted an agreement.

"But I suppose it could have been accidental."

"Doubtful."

I pulled back again, hating the coolness licking

over my bare skin after being cradled against his warmth for so long. Flutters woke in my belly over the possibility that he agreed with me. "Why do you say that?" I asked with a soft voice.

"Because I'm pretty sure he killed his last wife too."

20

Gideon

I let Addilyn digest that statement for a few seconds, her brow furrowed as she studied my face. "What makes you think he killed her?"

"He had a thing for my younger stepsister, and her mom found out."

She stared, blinking. "I-I wasn't the first?"

"I don't know if he ever really got his hands on her. She and her mom died of carbon monoxide poisoning while we were both conveniently out of town. I never called bullshit, but we'd shared enough knowing looks—and I can read Lloyd like a goddamn book."

"You can read everyone like a damn book," she muttered.

I snorted. *Used to.*

Somehow, he'd used my anger to manipulate me

into believing his lies. That fact pissed me the hell off.

Addilyn's gaze dropped to my lips, bringing me back to the present.

She was thinking about kissing me rather than the fucked up shit I'd just revealed. My ego preened a bit, enough to lessen my annoyance, but we weren't done with our sharing.

Especially the other shit I'd been able to read about those closest to her.

"Jenny was always jealous of you."

Addilyn's attention snapped up to my eyes.

"It's true," I continued. "She wanted Devon. Wanted me—and we both were hard for her best friend."

"She hurt me," Addilyn said, her voice husky and sexy as fuck from all the tears. "More emotionally than Lloyd ever could."

"What happened after I got locked up?"

Addilyn settled against me again, and my arms slid around her, my chin resting atop her head. "She came to the house to ask forgiveness, not that I would ever give it to her. We ended up fighting. I haven't talked to her since."

"What about school?"

"I finished out the year from home. That kept me on hand for Lloyd—"

"Fucker," I muttered, but she went on as though I hadn't interrupted.

"—but by fall, I looked forward to escaping the house for seven hours a day. I traded one hell for another, but at least no one touched me in school. No one spoke to me though. Devon and Jenny ended up dating for awhile, and fuck, did that ever sting."

My insides riled up. "You were upset he went out with her?"

She snorted a sarcastic laugh. "Absolutely not! Just embarrassed as hell. I wanted to sink into the floor every time I encountered them in the hallway."

"Did either of them talk to you again?"

"No."

I wasn't upset over that fact, but I sure as fuck hated the way she'd suffered. My insides clenched at how she must have shuffled through the hallways, books clasped to her chest, her focus on the floor. I couldn't imagine the anxiety she'd faced. The pain of having to live that shit over and over every goddamn day.

Jenny was a goddamn cunt of a girl. Disloyal. A backstabbing whore.

"I never wanted her," I muttered the truth.

Addilyn lay her hand on my chest like she'd done a half-dozen times, as though reassuring herself I was real, flesh and blood. "Back then, I thought maybe you did, and it made me green-eyed and cagey as hell."

I chuckled and scooched down on the bed so we

could lay side by side. "So, you're saying you always had a boner for me."

"My body did," she didn't hesitate to answer, "and I hated that my mind and heart did too."

"Why?"

"Because it was wrong, and you were a cocky jackass."

My smirk faded as I tucked her hair behind her ear. "I'm sorry for manipulating you that night. Making you get on your knees for me. You were so damn set on staying pure—"

"Purity was Mother's idea, not mine." My princess cut me off with snipped words. "Her ideals she'd tried to instill in me because of her own teenage years. At least, that's what I think. She wasn't religious. Never wanted to have kids of her own. I really don't know." She glanced over my shoulder to focus on the wall. "And now I never will."

"Does that upset you?"

She pondered for a few moments while I trailed my fingertips down her spine and back up again. "She was my mother. Not a good one, and definitely worse in the end to not believe me about Lloyd, but...she was still my mother."

"You're more gracious than me." I grunted, tugging her in tighter against me.

"I'll never forgive Jenny though."

"Any idea where she is and what she's up to these

days?” I had my reasons for asking, but Addilyn didn’t need to know about that sick part of my brain.

“Crack whore last I’d heard. Devon dumped her the night before prom our senior year. Broke her heart.”

“The whore part doesn’t surprise me. All she ever talked about was dick.”

Addilyn pulled back again to study my face, her gaze narrowing. “How many conversations of ours did you listen in on?”

I flashed my dimples. “All of them.”

That earned me another smack to my arm.

“And what about Devon?” I asked, rather than focusing on the fire in her eyes that would make my dick hard again.

“He’s studying law and is getting married this summer.”

“And what about you?”

“What about me?”

“Plans? Dreams? What’d I ruin by kidnapping you and hiding you away?”

I caught the smile on her lips before she tucked against my chest again. “Not a damn thing.”

A *good* fucking thing—because I had no intentions of letting her go back to the life she’d lived before my release.

She fell asleep not much later, but my mind refused to rest.

I'd gone through so much emotional upheaval in the previous two hours while she ruined her voice talking and crying. My heart ached for her, and rage simmered deep inside me. Lusting for revenge for her as well as me.

Needing it.

And I would have it, one goddamn soul at a time. Lloyd, I would save for last. Savor every second of the build up while he believed he had me and Addilyn where he wanted us.

Let him wait. Stir his anxiety by watching his best friend get tossed into the slammer. Sheriff Bradshaw would have his day thanks to Twinkie and his lover.

But Jenny and Devon…

I stewed on their names and where Addilyn had said they were in life as she slept in my arms. A crack whore and a soon-to-be husband. What better revenge could I have than taking them down together?

Addilyn wouldn't ever forgive Jenny—but would she try to stop me from being karma's bitch and making sure those two fuckfaces got what they deserved for hurting her?

Getting to Jenny would be laughably easy, but Devon would prove a tougher opponent. He studied law. Had a fiancée in his life. If I took down the sheriff first, he might be on guard.

Best to hit them both within a matter of hours.

That meant a trip down to Anchorage, which I had planned eventually anyway.

I slid from the bed, stripped down, and climbed back in beside Addilyn, ready to finally sleep.

But the fucking skin on skin beneath the quilt. Every inch of her pressed along me…

I closed my eyes and nosed against her hair, breathing her in. Lust stirred in my groin, but I forced my focus on detailing out the plan for the asshole and his old high school sweetheart to keep from fucking Addilyn awake.

They would pay.

And it wouldn't be pretty.

21

Addilyn

My mind roused to life, but warmth and contentment surrounded me, keeping me from opening my eyes. A heart beat against my ear. Sparse hair tickled my cheek. Hard muscle and hot skin rested beneath my hand.

An arm lay under my torso, a palm on my ass. One of my legs rested atop more prickling hair and hard muscle.

Gideon.

Longing rushed through me, and I lifted my head off his chest, blinking to bring him into focus.

Head propped up on a pillow, he watched me. Studied me with sleepy blue eyes void of anger, of bloodlust. Just…open. Vulnerable.

I shimmied up his torso and kissed him. Had to. I needed to taste his mouth without angst, to see if tenderness with him would turn me on like his anger did.

He groaned, his fingers sliding into my hair to hold me in place. Lips parting, he took over. Angled our heads. Ate at my mouth with tongue and teeth, morning breath be damned. Scruff scratched at my chin, and I rolled fully atop him, my core swelling with desire as I straddled his waist.

His dick lay hard as hell between us, and I rubbed myself against it. Chasing… Panting.

Holy hell, did he get me going. I never thought I'd feel arousal like that again—pure want.

"Gideon." I whispered my surprise at my body's reaction against his mouth.

He pushed me up to sit on his waist, his length trapped between us.

I gulped. Stared at the dips and swells of muscle from his shoulders down over massive pecs…ripples of abs. The dark trail of hair…the leaking tip of his hard dick peeking between us.

"You're wet."

My core pulsed at his ragged words, and I licked my suddenly dry lips while dragging my focus back up to his face.

Those eyes…good God, that look replaced any vulnerability. His head once more tipped back, he peered at me as though lava boiled inside him, ready to erupt and burn me to ash.

Gazes held, he shifted me back farther on his

thighs and grasped his dick. "You look like you want this—and I haven't even hurt you yet."

"Gideon," I whimpered his name, my focus falling to his hand which swirled up and over the head. Smearing pre-cum down his thick length, making his girth shiny and slick.

"Ride my dick, princess." He held it out toward me, same as he'd done once before, another droplet of pre-cum swelling.

"You wouldn't give it to me earlier because I *wanted* it." I tore my attention off what my tongue drooled for. "Why offer it freely now?"

A smirk curled a corner of his lip. "Because I went five years without a warm, wet hole to fuck, and now that I've had a taste of yours, I need more. Dreamt about it last night. Woke up tempted to shove my cock so damn far up your pussy you'd feel me in the back of your throat. Sit on my dick, princess. Make yourself come all over me."

"I-I won't come," I whispered what I knew to be true. Without pain, I wouldn't orgasm.

He grasped my neck again and yanked me close. Nose to nose. "I said climb aboard, princess."

His dick jerked, the back of it bumping against my clit.

I wanted it. Dripped for him again even before he'd wrapped his hand around my throat.

Lower lip between my teeth, I lifted. Shifted until his tip rested against me.

Gideon didn't thrust. Didn't move—simply grasped my neck firmly and held my gaze as though questioning what I waited for.

I lowered, and the notch of his flared head stung. Wincing, I paused.

"Do it, Addilyn," he commanded through gritted teeth. "Take every goddamn inch of my dick into your needy pussy like you've been dreaming about since you were fifteen years old."

Pressing down filled me with a lush burn, and I moaned, my hands clutching at the pillow on either side of his head.

Full. Stuffed completely full of throbbing, hot dick.

"Too much," I gasped, shifting my hips upward to escape the sting.

"Fuck…" Gideon grabbed my hip with his free hand and slid me down. Then forward, dragging my clit along his pelvis—it felt good. Real damn good. He showed me how to move. Back and forth. Rocking to fuck myself on his length. "Just. Like. That."

His hands fell away, and he rested his arms over-head, the muscles stretching and swelling all over the damn place. "Ride me," he commanded through gritted teeth.

I swallowed a flood of drool from the sight of him sitting back and waiting as though his dick alone could make me come.

"Cocky jackass."

"Fuck yourself on my dick, princess."

Shit, the words he said and the rumble of his low voice…

My body took control, and I slid over him like he'd shown me. Smooth glides, his length dragging along my walls and pressing back in with every shift of my hips.

"So fucking sexy." He stared at my swaying breasts, his hands fisting as though to keep from grabbing them.

I hadn't ever been in control when sleeping with a guy. Hadn't been on top, attempting to get someone off. Self-consciousness over my brokenness rose inside me, assurance that I wouldn't ever find release on my own.

"Touch me, Gideon," I begged while rocking over his too-thick length that hurt and made me wet at the same time. "Please."

He sat up and wrapped his arms around me, his mouth finding my hardened nipple. Steady strokes of his tongue, deep suckling, sent shots of need straight to my clit.

I couldn't ride in that position like he'd taught me, so I lifted and lowered on my knees, needing friction even though it stung…chasing the rub of his pelvis against my clit.

His tongue lashed, his teeth scraped, and his groans mingled with the wet sounds of our fucking.

The pain of him being inside me gave way to pure, torturous pleasure, the kind I'd fantasized about. Dreamed about. Exactly what I'd never expected to experience.

I moved faster, my insides fluttering, my breaths coming in pants. Rejuvenated by adrenaline and the warmth radiating throughout my body, I slammed myself down harder on his length.

So good. So very fucking good.

I grabbed hold of his head and clutched him to my chest, desperate for more. Ground my core against him, chasing the tingling in my belly that promised satiated bliss.

"Gideon…"

His hands found my ass. Squeezed and tugged. Fingertips dug in—but didn't bruise.

My thighs burned from lifting and lowering, and my insides shook as I hovered on the edge of climaxing.

Need pain...need more...

Gideon pulled back to lounge again and held my gaze, his thumb finding my clit. He shifted his hips and thrust up to meet me. Once. Twice. Without pain. Just spine-tingling pleasure.

"Oh…" I bit my lip, my entire body trembling. Grasping…reaching for what his stroking finger and insistent hips intended to give.

"Take it, Addilyn."

"Yes…oh yes!" I choked on a cry as my climax

swept over me, soaking his hand and his rippled abs. Every pulse throbbed my core around his thrusting length.

I smacked at his hand strumming my sensitive clit, but he refused to stop. Held my gaze, our souls seemingly entwined.

"Again, princess."

He made me come a second time, drenching him while I whimpered out his name, shuddering.

"Christ, Addilyn." Gideon grabbed hold of my hips and slammed me onto his dick, his eyes going dark, hazed with passion.

Heat erupted inside me, his throaty groan causing my skin to pebble.

"Oh God!" Another spasm rocked through me, and I ground against his groin like I couldn't get him deep enough.

"So fucking hot. Fuck, princess." He kneaded my ass cheeks, his length giving one last twitch inside me. Sanity returned to his eyes as his head tipped back to rest against the pillow while I struggled to fill my lungs.

"Jesus." He smirked, letting out a chuckle while heaving for breath. "Told you."

"Jackass."

Within a blink, my back met the mattress, my pussy empty.

Gideon knelt between my legs, his focus between my thighs.

His cum oozed from my core, and he smeared it all over my lower lips, my clit—down over my asshole.

I flinched, my stomach tightening.

He lifted his gaze to my face, his fingertip rimming my hole. "Did that fuckface take you here?"

"Yes," I whispered on a gasp, hating that my skin crawled, that I wanted to slam my thighs closed against Gideon's gentle touch. Lloyd hadn't been anything but harsh when he'd stolen that part of my innocence, and I hadn't allowed anyone touch me there since.

"Did you come?"

"N-No."

"Mmm." Gideon kept my eyes ensnared with his, slick finger still sliding around my puckered hole I clenched tight. Back and forth. Teasing, almost feeling—good. "Whose hands are on you, princess?"

I let out a breath I hadn't realized I'd held, all thoughts of Lloyd fleeing from the tingles sweeping across my skin over Gideon's feather-light caresses. My hole relaxed beneath his touch. "You are."

"I'm going to own this ass one day," Gideon said, applying light pressure, just enough to slide painlessly up to the first knuckle inside my body. "And you're going to let me, aren't you?" he asked, holding still.

I opened my mouth to say yes but hesitated,

considering the push and pull between us. The pain of feigned violence that promised pleasure. "No."

The glint lighting his eyes sent a rush of flat-out lust straight through my body, and I hopped aboard the idea of him sliding his finger deeper inside me, readying me for something four times its girth.

"No?"

I shook my head, chin lifting.

"We'll see about that, princess."

The jackass winked, pulled his finger from my ass, and climbed off the bed, leaving me feeling... empty. Like I'd lost out. I frowned at his back as he sauntered from the bedroom, even though the hollowness in my chest I'd lived with for the previous five years had filled.

With him. His scent. His touch.

I sank into the mattress with a shuddering exhale, and my furrowed brow eased, my lips tipping upward.

At least he hadn't locked me in.

22

Gideon

"Why did you bring me here, Gideon?"

We sprawled on the bed after eating a couple cans of stew. Naked. Skin on skin—sated for a while—so talk time, it was.

"I planned to break you for your part in putting me away. I hated you because of what Lloyd told me. He played me, and when I got out of jail, he was there with all the intel I needed on you. He also offered me money to help him get you back."

Addilyn's fingertips that refused to stop touching me, stilled. "You were really going to take me for him?"

"Only to fuck with him. I would have you. Break you—then break him by denying him access to you."

"You were going to kill me?"

I frowned up at the ceiling, recognizing and

admitting the truth to myself—I never would've been able to spill enough blood for her to bleed out. "I'd thought about it, but making you suffer pleased me more."

"What changed your mind?"

Shifting, I faced her, lifting her leg over my hip and opening her body to mine. "Your innocence in all this. Finding out you wanted me. That you lived with shame and depression for five years."

Wetness coated her eyes as she held my gaze, that connection I'd always felt to her swirling around my heart and filling me with an overflow of emotion I didn't know how to handle.

"You've done enough suffering, princess, and I wish to God you never had."

Our lips came together, and I breathed her in, my blood simmering at the sweet taste of her. The grasp of her hands at my shoulder, my hair, telling me she felt the same as I slid my dick into her wet core.

Always so fucking wet…

Fuck.

Slow and steady, we fucked, our mouths fused, soaking in each other and touching and tasting until she pulled back, her gaze too clear—too fucking on point while stuffed full of my dick.

"What?" I asked, pressing in until her womb stopped me from thrusting deeper.

She lifted her leg higher over my hip to give me

better access when a frown dented her brow. "Did you have a plan for him too?"

Lloyd.

Why the fuck was she thinking about him while my dick owned what he'd wanted for himself?

Addilyn continued to shift with every slow thrust of my hips I couldn't stop regardless of the sudden topic.

What the fuck ever. At least her pussy was wrapped around my cock.

"I wanted to ruin him financially, leave him with nothing," I said, shoving fully into her. "But after hearing what he did to you?" I thrust again, holding her gaze, keeping her with me in the present. "Fuck mercy," I whispered harshly. "I'm going to end him."

Her pupils swelled, like the thought of me spilling my own fucking father's blood turned her on. "Good."

Getting aroused by my promise to take his life? Addilyn Reed couldn't be any more perfect, and that truth sent adrenaline rushing through me, made pre-cum ooze all over the insides of her pussy.

"I thought you'd talk me out of it," I said, withdrawing and sliding right the fuck back into heaven, my balls drawing up over her wet heat clasping at me.

She snorted, grinding her hips to take me deeper. "After the horror he put me through...he doesn't deserve to live." Addilyn pressed close to me, sinking her teeth into my lower lip until the coppery tang of blood hit my tongue.

My dick jerked inside her, and I let out a groan as she lapped at the wetness she'd caused.

"Just make it hurt first," she whispered against my mouth.

"Fuck, princess." I thrusted and throbbed, her desire for blood heating mine. "I will—count on it."

"I want to be there." She licked my lower lip again, her body writhing in my hold as I chased the rush tingling in my balls.

This fucking woman…her tits jiggled with every slam of my hips.

"I want to see him powerless. Hopeless." She grunted, eyes glazing over at how harshly I took her. "I want to hear him beg for you to stop torturing him."

"Fuck, yes."

"He needs to beg for his life," she continued, grasping at my hair. "And I want to look into his eyes as the life fades from him."

"Hearing you say shit like that…Jesus." I held her tight against me and slammed against her womb. Cum fucking erupted, and I grunted and groaned with every pulse shooting from my aching balls to coat her insides.

"Fuck." I blinked her into focus while catching

my breath. "You're one hell of a woman, Addilyn, making me cum like a goddamn kid."

She squeezed her pussy around my flagging dick. "Wanting those things doesn't make me sick?"

"I just filled you full of cum while talking about killing the man who gave me life. Who's the sick fuck?"

She didn't answer, so I pulled from her body's warm clasp, shoved her onto her back, and showed her what *sick* was by licking her clean of my own cum and fingering her sore pussy until she drenched the mattress beneath us.

***

For three days, we ate, slept, and fucked. Showered —and fucked in there too. Addilyn got on her knees for me and choked on my dick while water sluiced over my body, reminding me so much of the first time that I damn near blew early like an untried teenager.

Fucking Addilyn...my sweet princess. Claimed she didn't want my dick just to get me to fuck her rough and ragged. Begged for it if I tried to savor every second and made her wait.

I forgot my goddamn name while balls deep inside her body. Until she called it out while soaking my dick—then I'd go and forget it again while emptying.

When I wasn't losing myself in her, we talked about my plans and morphed them when ideas came to her.

Like Bonny and Clyde come back to life, we planned our rampage, but unlike them, we wouldn't end up riddled with bullets.

She had money of her own, or would once her birthday came to pass, so no bank robbing lay on our to-do list.

I just needed to keep her safe until that time.

Lloyd continued to text, and I finally answered, telling him she'd broken but I hadn't yet had my fill of exacting revenge on her ass. A lie, but what the fuck ever. I'd been the one to break and couldn't give a flying fuck over that fact.

I had my princess back, one who liked to get snippy and claw me with her fingernails whenever the mood to fuck struck.

She came countless times, regardless of pain. Just pure, fucking pleasure. I didn't need to get into her head—I could tell with every fuck, every kiss, every caress that I erased more of the bad memories. Pink returned to her cheeks and a healthy flush to her torso that didn't appear quite as gaunt as before.

We sat at the table, eating steaks I'd pan-fried in a cast-iron skillet atop the fire. Baked potatoes with salt and a can of corn completed our feast.

"Shit this tastes so good it should be illegal," I

muttered, shoving the final bite of steak between my teeth, my focus on the glow of her face.

She lifted her legs up, feet on the chair, and pulled my T-shirt over her knees. "They didn't serve you real food in prison?"

I snorted. "Fuck no."

"So shitty food, no women, obviously." She studied my face while I chewed. "Did you…"

"Fuck no," I stated again.

"Five years is a long time to go without anything other than your fist."

I eyed her while wiping my mouth over my sleeve. She wanted to talk about jail? Knowing the truth of the animal I'd become would probably bring out the hissing cat desperate to escape me. My dick twitched at the challenge.

"I shanked three fuckers while in there."

"Shanked?"

I picked up my steak knife and stabbed the air, watching her face. "Shed blood. Ended lives."

Her eyes didn't widen, lips didn't part.

"You aren't surprised." But I sure as fuck was over her lack of it.

"I've seen your rage," she stated with a shrug like it was no big deal I'd killed three guys.

"And you don't despise it? Don't think I deserve to rot in hell for what I've done?" I sure as fuck didn't. Assholes like the ones I ended didn't deserve to live, and I took karma's place once again.

Addilyn chewed on her lower lip. "I know it's not right," she finally said, "but I kinda get like when you lose your shit. Watching the video in the courtroom that day, seeing you beat Devon…" The pulse in her neck kicked up, and she licked her lower lip.

My princess got off on the same shit I did.

"You're one sick bitch," I said with a laugh, my swelling dick requiring an adjustment.

Her gaze dropped to her plate, her brow furrowing. "I know," she whispered.

Ah, shit.

"Hey." I reached over the table and grasped her chin, lifting her focus to me. "I didn't mean it like that."

Her goddamn eyes welled. "Then how did you mean it, Gideon? Watching you beat Devon to hell turned me on. Pain arouses me. I'm not horrified you killed three guys—knowing you, they probably deserved it, but that doesn't excuse how your violence makes me feel. There's no other word to describe it *but* sick."

"You're fucking perfect." I pulled her up and over the table like she weighed next to nothing, shoved back my chair, and settled her on my lap. My possessiveness knew no bounds. "I wouldn't have you any other way, Addilyn Jane Reed. So damn soft." I kissed her lips, wishing she could feel the pride swelling in my chest. "Sexy." I nipped her lower lip. "Full of fire and spit—I fucking love when you fight me. Make me hard so I can fuck you until you squirt all over me."

"Gideon," she moaned against my mouth, grinding against my rigid length trapped between us. "All we do is fuck."

I pulled back and narrowed my gaze. "You got me locked up for five years without pussy and have the balls to complain I want yours every hour of the goddamn day?" I asked without an ounce of heat even though the idea of punishing her stirred up my lust to full on throbbing.

"I'm sorry." No tears—she fucking knew what I meant.

I shoved to a stand, toppling my chair over. Three strides put me beside the couch, and I whipped the little princess around, shoving her over the back. An upward swipe bunched the T-shirt at her nape.

That ass…

Teeth gritting, I swung, my palm stinging over her cheek.

"Ow!" She shrieked and tried to pull away, but I gripped her hair tight and landed another smack.

Lloyd hadn't ever hit her—I'd fucking asked so I wouldn't bring up shit that would break her mind.

I'd wanted to ruin her more than anything, but after claiming her sweet body…my nature refused to let my rage win.

Three more swats and she stopped fighting, letting out a low moan.

Couldn't have that either.

I pressed my aching dick against her ass and yanked her upper body back. My teeth found her earlobe, and I bit. Hard.

She shuddered, and I chuckled, nuzzling along her neck that smelled like sex—and me. My princess was the most goddamn potent aphrodisiac on the planet. I had to have her again, but I wanted her heart racing, her pupils blown with fear.

"Run," I whispered and released her.

A yelp and she leaped away, knocking over the lamp on the end table as her hip bashed into it. She didn't slow but took a few running steps into the kitchen.

I stalked after her, ripping my shirt over my head. Unbuttoning my jeans.

Kicked off my shoes as she screeched and ran around the table.

Her eyes gleamed when I shoved down my jeans and let them lay where they fell on the floor.

I raced back into the living area—around the couch—and I feigned heading one way before stepping into her path and catching her going the other.

Over the couch's back she went again, fighting to escape me, limbs flying, but I trapped her down, my hand fumbling between her shifting thighs.

Fucking soaked.

"Jesus fucking Christ, princess."

"Get your fingers out of me!"

I shoved in a third.

"Get off me!"

Groaning, I twisted my wrist and found the roughened patch that would give me what I wanted. I fucked her hard, my dick jerking as she squirted with every harsh rub of my fingertips deep inside her.

"Fucking...stop it!"

Pressing her chest down, I crowded in close while pulling my fingers free. I sucked my lower lip between my teeth, knowing what waited for me— and drove myself home into her slick pussy. "Ah, fuck..."

Pulling back, I eyed her ass, my soaked fingers sliding over the puckered hole I'd been lusting for.

"No!"

"Yes, princess," I growled, rimming my finger around it—giving her a few seconds to stop me for real.

She thrashed. Cursed me. But my dick stayed buried in her pussy, and I slipped a finger past the ring of muscle inside her ass without resistance.

Her hot heat clamped down on my knuckles, and I groaned as my balls tightened.

"G-Gideon..." Addilyn shuddered and tried to shift away from me, but I held her still. Fucked her ass gently, slowly with my finger, my hips holding her in place while she was impaled on my dick.

A tug on her hair pulled her upright, but she arched, sticking her tits out. I added a second finger to her ass, drawing a deep moan from her that vibrated through her back into my chest.

"So fucking hot," I breathed against her ear, my dick ready to blow. "Tell me I can have this, Addilyn," I told her while scissoring my fingers, opening her ass up for me. "I won't take it unless you tell me I can."

"Yes."

The only fucking time I liked that goddamn word.

My insides tight and ready to blow, I pulled out of her pussy and pressed the throbbing head of my dick against her puckered hole. "Push back and let me in—" The command didn't even finish on my lips before she obeyed. Slick from her arousal and my pre-cum, I slid in a few inches without resistance.

"O-oh God. Gideon…"

Her ass choked my goddamn dick.

"Christ." I swore while backing out—sank in again with another groaned curse aimed at God and all things fucking holy. Squeezing her cheeks, I spread them wide. Dug my fingers into her soft flesh while pulling out again, her hot hole sucking at my girth.

Addilyn whimpered. Shifted beneath me. "H-hurt me," she whispered on a choked sob.

Yeah, I'd get right on that shit, but first…

I slid back in, groaning as she took another two inches of me.

Almost fucking there.

After another slow drag out, my eyes were damn near ready to roll from my head. "So fucking hot, princess. God, your ass is strangling my dick…" My balls tingled, but I pushed in. Fully. Damn eyes rolled back into my head as I shuddered, pausing to calm myself.

Fucking finally. How many times had I jerked off imagining claiming her ass for my own? But she felt better than any fantasy. Hotter. Tighter.

"Jesus…" Buried deep, my dick throbbed, on the verge of release. I squeezed her cheeks, studying how her pink hole stretched around my girth. "You're goddamn perfect."

"Gideon. P-please."

"I've got you, princess." I backed away, teeth gritted—and slammed into her so hard we moved the couch a few inches.

"Ah!" Addilyn cried out. Sobbed my name like a goddamn prayer.

I plowed into her again. "Like that? Hmm?" Another deep thrust and I bent my legs for a better angle. Fucked into her so hard she shrieked.

"More," she gasped as I pulled out, leaving only my swollen head inside her tight heat.

I leaned over her back, licking up her spine. Salt and sweat. Fucking delicious. "You want my dick?"

"Mmmhmm."

I breathed against her ear. "Fight me for it."

She did, her fingernails grasping at my wrists where I clenched her ass cheeks. Drew fucking blood…bucked beneath me like a damn animal, hissing and shrieking. Cursing. Moaning.

"Gonna fill your ass up with my cum," I told her, my balls ready to detonate from fucking her without mercy.

"Yes—oh, fuck, yes," she sobbed, every inch of her shimmering with sweat and glinting in the firelight in front of her.

"Play with your clit. Come while I fuck your ass."

"C-can't."

I shoved a hand between her hips and the couch —damn near bruising my wrist—but I found her swollen nub. Thrusting, I leaned over her, my teeth on her neck, my fingertips plucking. Pinching.

"G-Gideon…"

"Yeah. Oh, fuck yeah. Squirt all over my hand, princess."

"Fuck!" She shrieked. Shuddered—and came with a rush, her release dripping off my sack and onto the floor.

I grunted with each thrust, the build-up in my balls ready to erupt.

Needing to mark her, needing to see she belonged to me, I pulled out. Fisted my dick. Two hard tugs and I shot all over her ass and the red prints I'd left behind.

Gasping for breath, I rubbed my spunk into her skin while she lay there, dead to the world. "So fucking good," I panted, squeezing her sticky ass. Slapping to make it jiggle.

So fucking mine.

23

Addilyn

"Where have you been?" Ciarra threw her arms around me, hugging me tight.

I'd used Gideon's throwaway cell phone to call her the day before we attempted the drive through the melting snow into the city. We'd gotten a hotel room at a dive north of Anchorage, a home base of sorts to hide out in until we saw our plans through.

Step one had been for me to get into contact with my only friend. I hadn't given her more than the name of the hotel and asked her to come see me and take care to not be followed.

The second Gideon had opened the door and stepped back, Ciarra had come barreling in.

"I've been worried sick!"

I hugged her hard, my eyes stinging even though relief over the sight of her swelled inside me. Rather than answering, I pulled back. "I want you to meet someone."

Watching her closely, Gideon moved our way.

She turned to face him. "You're Gideon." Ciarra didn't even need the introduction as she glanced down over him. Guess I'd described him to a fault.

He wore those jeans of his and the boots that made him look badass. A gray T-shirt hugged the mass of his upper body, and I salivated even though I'd licked down every inch of him the night before when we finally arrived it to our hotel room.

"And you're Ciarra," he rumbled his reply, lips flatlined, eyes void of emotion.

Her gaze narrowed as she strained her neck to stare at him like she could read his intentions toward me. I'd always been short, but my friend? She looked like a midget next to Gideon.

She must have come to a positive conclusion, because Ciarra turned her focus me without railing into him. "There are so many rumors going around. His release. Your disappearance. Everyone thinks he killed you."

"Just kidnapped."

Her glare jerked back toward Gideon again. "What's going on? And I want the truth. That bitch Jenny betrayed her trust, but Addilyn knows I never would."

I met Gideon's gaze. He waited. Gave me the

chance to make the final decision we'd discussed but hadn't concluded.

"Gideon?" I questioned him one last time.

He nodded.

"Lloyd asked him to do away with me before my twenty-first birthday."

"So he could claim your money," Ciarra didn't hesitate to complete the why—without a shiver. "Dick. I *knew* someone was following us!"

"But Gideon and I figured out Lloyd had lied to both of us," I went on, sinking onto the bed's edge. She settled beside me, and Gideon leaned against the wall, arms crossed which made all his muscles pop out.

Luscious. His face didn't so much as twitch, but his eyes were hooded as he tilted his head back, watching me.

Jackass.

I tore my stare off him. "He manipulated both of us. So instead of giving me to that asshole, Gideon is going to take me away from here for a while to keep me safe. I won't be back until after my birthday. I'll live to see that day because I have my protector with me again."

"You'll inherit everything your mother left to you," Ciarra added, "and Lloyd gets nothing."

"Exactly."

Ciarra smirked, a glint in her eye. "Talk about ruthless revenge!"

I huffed a laugh while pushing away the guilt over telling her a half-truth. She had no idea about the rest of the shit we wanted to do to my rapist. Hopefully, he didn't see or catch wind of us being in the city.

That would fuck everything up.

"So, who is this guy, exactly?" I asked as Gideon drove us southward into Anchorage the next evening after being shut up in our hotel room all day. Twilight already covered the land thanks to the Alaskan winter, and I felt like we headed into even deeper darkness with what we had planned.

Gideon's gaze flicked from rearview to side mirrors and back again.

Always watchful.

"Roger's nephew," he finally answered me. "Eugene. Don't know much else."

"And you're sure the evidence on that flash drive is enough to put Devon's father away?"

"Positive. Rogers wouldn't lie. The shit he's suffered because of his supposed friend, partner in crime—he'd slice Bradshaw's neck given the chance."

"I'm surprised he didn't just ask you to do it for him," I said, glancing out the windshield as we entered a part of the city I was well acquainted with.

Mere blocks from the university. We passed the pizzeria Leo and I had gone to.

It seemed ages ago. How I thought I could ever be with someone other than Gideon...

"Rogers wants the sheriff locked up with him so he can do the deed himself."

"What's on the drive?" I asked.

"Pictures. Phone recordings. Falsified records of evidence. Copies of emails. All of it will prove Sheriff Bradshaw was just as crooked as his partner in crime."

"Partner being Rogers, right?"

"Yep. Devon's dad framed his buddy, had him arrested before Rogers had a chance to retrieve the evidence."

"Why didn't his lawyer just get it and take it to court to prove his innocence?"

"A rich friend paid off Rogers's defense team." Gideon glanced at me, his eyes suggesting I make a guess. Connect the dots.

"Lloyd," I breathed what had to be true.

"Yep. Sheriff wasn't the only one benefitting from confiscated evidence. Lloyd was always a gambler. Out for a quick buck, and he didn't mind spending if it meant a possible return. Keeping Bradshaw from jail meant more possible shit for him to sell off and profit from."

"Asshole," I muttered. "I'm meeting this Eugene guy," I stated, ready to put up a fight if Gideon denied me. "I'm seeing this shit through to the very end with you."

He reached over and laced his fingers through my chilled ones. "Wouldn't have it any other way, princess."

I relaxed, warm fuzzies in my belly making me smile. "So, where are we going?"

"Dive diner. A few blocks away."

We slid into an old booth a few minutes later, fifties music of all things muffled in the background. Only a handful of people sat drinking coffee and eating pie, and I shifted on my seat across from Gideon. He faced the door, waiting for Eugene, the one who held the ticket to our revenge on Sheriff Bradshaw. A winter hat covered his head and ears, three days' worth of whiskers helping to hide his identity in case Lloyd had people looking for us. I wore the same, my white-blonde hair tucked up beneath.

"How do you know this guy won't turn on you?" I asked quietly as the waitress moved off with our order for water and chamomile tea.

"He doesn't know what's on the drive. Can't access it without the password," Gideon replied, his gaze over my shoulder without a doubt plastered to the door.

"Why didn't Rogers just have Eugene hand over the evidence?"

"He didn't know who he could trust. How far the deception went, who all was involved."

"So you're saying this could be dangerous."

He glanced at me, focus flitting over my eyes before settling on my flatlined lips. "Could be, but we're getting the evidence to someone outside this city. Outside of the sheriff's reach."

"FBI?"

Gideon smirked. "Smart girl." He lifted his focus behind me once more, his gaze hardening. "The fuck?"

I glanced over my shoulder.

"Addilyn?" Hazel eyes met mine.

I turned back to Gideon as he rose to his feet, his face blank.

"Leo." I hopped up too, taking a step toward my friend. We shared an awkward hug, and surprisingly, Gideon didn't make a sound or punch Leo out.

"Where have you been?" he asked, stepping away from me and taking a quick look at the mountain of a man behind me.

"Long story—but I'm fine," I told him with a shaky smile, thankful Gideon hadn't let his protective nature rage. "Good, actually."

He studied my face for a few seconds before his split into a goofy grin. "I can tell."

"So, hot date?" I asked, elbowing him and lifting my eyebrows.

"Not really, no." Leo glanced at Gideon again. "I'm here to meet someone…Gideon?"

"Eugene?"

Leo cringed but nodded. "I go by Leo, but yeah."

Holy hell, what are the chances?

Gideon leaned forward and offered his hand—shaking Leo's like a gentleman.

My eyeballs about popped from their sockets. Studying Gideon's passive face, I slid back into the booth, and he moved in beside me rather than across like he'd been.

Leo took Gideon's previous seat and pulled the flash drive from his back pocket. "Care to tell me what all this is about?" he asked, glancing between the two of us. "You just up and disappear without a trace for weeks, and suddenly you're with the man the newspapers said you helped put away."

I glanced up at Gideon, my hands clasped tightly on my lap, not sure how to reply.

He didn't take his focus off of Leo. "It's classified."

Leo snorted a laugh. "You sound like Uncle."

Gideon actually smirked and held out his hand for the evidence. "If all goes well, your uncle will be home soon."

Leo sobered, staring at Gideon. "You knew him in jail."

Gideon nodded.

"And there's something on here that's going to get him freed."

A quick tap to Gideon's nose had Leo sliding the flash drive across the table. "A simple call to tell me he'd hidden it in my old teddy bear and I could have taken this to the police for him."

"Too many hands in the pot," Gideon stated, tucking the flash drive away in his coat pocket. "He doesn't want you caught up in it."

Gideon had gotten what he wanted—would he smash in Leo's nose now? I bit my lower lip, trying not to shift on the plastic bench. While I liked my protector's blood rage, I didn't want him to hurt my friend.

"Why didn't he have someone else get this from me?" Leo asked before Gideon could make a move. "Someone on the outside?"

"Your uncle isn't a trusting man."

Leo glanced between us, sitting back in the booth as though to create distance. "And yet he would put his fate in the hands of a convict?"

Gideon leaned onto the table but without the tension riding him that promised pain. "He *knows* I have his back." His tone didn't betray a hint of doubt.

I studied Gideon while the two men held a stare down contest. Gideon had admitted to shanking a few guys while in jail. Had he spilled blood in defense of Leo's uncle? Such an action would solidify the kind of trust Gideon spoke of.

"Okay." Leo finally nodded and slid off the

booth's seat to stand. "If he trusts you, then I do too. Looking forward to seeing him."

"You will." Gideon nodded. "Just as soon as I get this evidence where it needs to go."

Gideon climbed from the booth—so I followed.

The waitress questioned us as we walked past her with our drinks. We didn't stop. Gideon didn't acknowledge her.

I shrugged with a mouthed, "Sorry?" while following Gideon out into the night, ready for the next step in our plan for revenge.

24

Gideon

Thank fuck I hadn't offed the Devon lookalike that night in the pizzeria parking lot.

Eugene. Leo. The prick Addilyn had gone out with.

I side-eyed her while driving north toward the library. She sat primly, hands on her lap, gazing out the passenger window as though deep in thought.

If she knew how close I'd come to sinking my knife into Leo's throat, soaking the ground with his blood…

A muscle ticked in my jaw, and I clenched the steering wheel tighter, my focus on the road. He'd hugged her. Put his fucking arms around what belonged to me. And I'd held onto my goddamn sanity by a mere thread, knowing I would lose out on my revenge if I dismembered the little fucker.

I filled my lungs fully to the count of eight and let the breath escape in a quiet, slow exhale past my parted lips.

It had been Addilyn's idea to go to the library rather than her house to make paper copies of the information on the stick. Better to be safe than sorry, she'd said, and I agreed since Lloyd wouldn't be caught dead in a library.

We sat in silence, scrolling through the evidence. Printing out the shit that the sheriff wouldn't be able to deny and getting the address of a local FBI agent who'd moved to Alaska three weeks earlier. And I hunched in front of the computer while she made a trip to the bathroom.

A quick search gave me the address I needed.

Addilyn didn't know about my plans for her old boyfriend and the little cunt who'd broken my princess's trust. She might get turned on by gruesome thoughts of paying Lloyd back for what he'd done to her, but I doubted she would approve of what I had in store for the others.

But the sheriff would pay first.

A few hours later, I slid the thick manila envelope stuffed full of evidence through the agent's mail slot, rang his doorbell, and hurried away into the night, hat tucked low over my head and shoulders hitched against the cold.

Slipping behind a tree, I glanced further up the road where my old Subaru waited. I couldn't make out Addilyn in the front seat, but I could feel her eyes on me.

The house's door opened, and I peeked from the tree's darkness. Eyed the guy looking up and down the street, envelope in his hands. Breath held, I watched and waited. He glanced at the envelope, flipping it over.

I hadn't bothered writing his name. Had Addilyn keep on her small mittens while gathering the papers up from the library's printer and putting them in the envelope. I too wore gloves while delivering the evidence. Couldn't have fingerprints on a goddamn thing.

While I would have loved for the sheriff to know uncovering his sins had been my doing, I couldn't have anything pointing back at me. One hint of exacting my revenge could lead to another stint in jail—but for murder.

I had too much to look forward to. A life ahead of me, one with a woman I would kill for—fucking die for. Nothing would keep us from living out my dream.

Nothing.

The FBI agent turned back into his house and shut the door with a click that echoed through the cold air.

My breath left in a rush, a puff of white.

Fucking cold had returned with a vengeance. I hurried up the road.

I yanked off my gloves and blew my breath onto my hands once enclosed in the car's warm interior with her.

"Now what?" Addilyn asked quietly.

"Now we cross our fingers that agent will do the right thing and wait for the outcome." I put the car into drive and pulled away from the curb. It could take days. Weeks. How long before Lloyd hired someone to come after us? Or had he already?

He wouldn't be able to find us at the cabin, but the hotel? Every time we went out, we risked being seen no matter how careful we were.

"We're going to grab our shit and head north," I said, my mind made up. "We're already pressing our luck by being in the city. Waiting here for the shit to hit the fan means a greater chance of running into Lloyd."

But I would return.

Without Addilyn.

She'd be pissed, but I couldn't take any chances. I had plans that didn't include her, and no way in fucking hell would I let her stop me.

"I think we should stay."

I glanced at her. "Every minute we're here—"

"I know," she cut me off, angling to face me. "But I want to see that asshole get hauled off in cuffs, Gideon. Just like you. At the cabin, there's no TV. No newspapers."

She had a point, but I needed her back at

Twinkie's where she would be safe while I finished cleaning up the mess of my past.

Lloyd was too invested in his dead wife's money —and daughter. No fucking way he'd run even if he did suspect I had a hand in getting his friend locked up.

But would he trust me enough to follow me once I contacted him with the lie that Addilyn had finally broken? Would he allow me to see my plan to fruition?

If not, I would think of another plan to get him where I needed him to be.

"One week," I stated, hating that I gave in.

"Two."

A muscle ticked in my jaw. Two put us too damn close to her birthday, but I finally nodded. Two weeks, max. And on day thirteen, if we still sat in the hotel awaiting justice for Sheriff Bradshaw, I would have to move forward—whether Addilyn wanted it or not.

25

Addilyn

Days passed in seclusion.

We fucked. Ate take out.

Made up for lost time by fucking some more. Every night, I lay sated, bow-legged and exhausted. Sweaty and dripping cum from my abused pussy or ass. Gideon fucked like an animal. Rough and bruising, the pain so exquisite I often cried.

He licked my tears, told me how much he craved and jacked off to them. Showed me how hard they made his dick.

His filthy words of how my sickness turned him on only got me wetter. Needier.

Would I ever come to terms with the darkness inside me? Could I accept the depraved woman I'd become because of Gideon—and Lloyd? There was no denying my stepfather had some part in twisting my body, my mind, in what turned me on.

As an innocent, I had desired things I shouldn't. Reality had proved more horrific because being taken by force had been so very wrong, regardless of how my body responded.

With each passing day, I questioned who I was, what I was. How any normal, sane person could enjoy violence and blood, bruising fingertips and slapping palms…filthy words that would have at one time reddened my face and made my insides squirm.

Pretending to not want Gideon while soaked for him just to give us both a thrill…it didn't sit right in my head, no matter how much the actions made my body purr. And when he left me twice to get us essentials and some supplies, I missed him. Ached for him. He returned the first time with my laptop and a bag of my clothes.

A present, he'd called them.

Rustled together after a quick call to my old roommate who I longed to see again.

He denied me, the jackass.

We couldn't take the chance of her being trailed, couldn't take any more chances than we already did —but I still lusted for him even while pissed off. Longed for his hands on my body, his marks on my skin. My fingers itched to scrape him up with my nails. Make him bleed.

I did.

Sunday morning, almost two weeks since arriving in Anchorage, the morning news anchor on the local station announced some breaking news which ended our time in the city.

The sheriff had been arrested.

I hurried out of the bathroom, drying my wet hair with a towel. Gideon sat on the bed's edge, naked and hot, his eyes hard and focused on the TV.

Devon's dad was being taken out of their house in handcuffs by the FBI. Head lowered, shoulders slumped. He didn't carry himself with his usual arrogance. No smirk on his face.

Vicious satisfaction at seeing him led away like he'd done to Gideon coursed through me…how did Gideon sit so unmoved?

New evidence, the anchor said, none of which had yet been released, but another arrest had been made in the scandal from years earlier…there must be good reason, the anchor continued.

I turned back toward Gideon.

He still stared at the TV, lips flatlined.

"Poetic justice," I stated, dropping the towel and climbing on his lap to straddle his thighs.

He met my gaze, a glint in his eye.

"Cuffed on a Sunday morning—just like you." I smoothed back his hair, smiling softly. "Are you happy?"

"I will be once he's behind bars and Rogers takes his own revenge."

Butterflies lit in my belly, excitement and arousal. I leaned in and kissed Gideon, thinking we needed to celebrate.

The jackass set me aside and stood. "It's time to get out of town."

I frowned. Gideon never turned me away when I came looking for his mouth or his dick. "Are you okay?"

"Yeah." He strode into the bathroom and shut the door.

Had seeing the video clip brought back memories from when he'd been arrested?

I'd expected a good, hard celebratory fuck, but something had upset him enough to not want me.

Chewing on my lower lip, I considered his coldness, his lack of action. What was I missing? Had he been full of shit in saying he'd never get enough of me? Of my hot, tight ass?

I went to the closed door. "Gideon?" I called.

"Get your shit together, princess. We're leaving in five."

Bossy asshole.

I scowled at the door, my hands on my hips. Maybe he needed time to digest what he'd set into motion. Maybe he didn't feel the relief, the satisfaction he'd expected and was disappointed.

Or maybe he'd gotten what he'd wanted from me. My body, my pain…and a part of my heart.

I pushed that thought away while pulling on

some clothes. Not once had Gideon mentioned any of the emotions he felt toward me. Everything between us had always been physical. We hadn't spoken of the connection we shared whenever our gazes clashed with understanding.

But I'd felt that shit. Had to trust in it because I had nothing else. Losing Gideon would be like… I had nothing to compare it to. Couldn't imagine no longer experiencing what I did when I was with him.

Even if it was sick.

Ten minutes later, we headed up the highway, and Gideon remained quiet and broody. I couldn't handle the silence between us while my mind continued to question.

"What's wrong?" I asked, my stomach a hard knot.

He glanced in the rearview mirror. "Nothing."

"Bullshit."

I didn't even get a side eye.

"Talk to me, Gideon. Tell me what's going on in that head of yours."

"Nothing you need to worry about."

I glared at him, hating his bland tone that only twisted my belly up tighter. He could read me like an open book, but beyond the occasional hint of vulnerability he'd allowed through the first couple of months, I realized I didn't know him.

Not really.

"Talk to me," I repeated.

"I'd rather not."

I hugged myself and peered out over the white landscape of the cold wilderness. The weather had warmed up a bit, enough to melt some of the snow, but winter still clung. Frigid. Biting.

"I thought we were in this together," I muttered, sounding like a whiny brat, but it was preferable than revealing the ache in my chest if he hoped to hurt me like I feared.

"We are, but there are some things best left in the dark."

I glanced at him, somewhat mollified by his assurance that we were of the same mind, but the tension riding me didn't relent. "Why can't I know what you're thinking, Gideon? What do you have planned that you aren't telling me?"

"Do you trust me?"

I studied his profile, wondering why the hell he would even ask such a thing—and yet questioning in the deepest parts of me if I actually did. "Of course I do." I stated what I wanted to be the truth. What I longed for.

But I wondered if *he* trusted *me* after what I'd done to him.

I couldn't bear the idea of asking and having him remain silent.

So I kept my mouth shut the rest of the ride into the wilderness.

26

Gideon

ddilyn slept on our tiny bed. It'd taken a two-hour long fucking session to finally shut her the fuck up. Once we got back to the cabin, she'd poked and prodded me for my thoughts and my emotions over what we'd made happen to that point, but I didn't even know myself. Couldn't explain what I had no words for.

I wasn't happy. Wasn't relieved.

Not yet.

I tucked the quilt up beneath her chin, and she didn't shift. Her steady breaths didn't disrupt thanks to the chamomile tea I'd made for her an hour earlier.

When this is over, I'll feel something. I'll have words for you then.

If she even allowed me to speak to her after drugging her a second time. She'd wake like a bitch from hell, hungover and pissed off at me, but at least she wouldn't be tied and blindfolded.

I slipped from the bedroom, leaving the door open behind me. A fire roared in the fireplace. It'd taken a couple hours to heat the cabin, but by dinner we'd been comfortable. Since I'd drained the water lines and put antifreeze in the toilet and down the sink traps before we'd gone into town, none of the pipes had frozen in our absence.

Something Twinkie and I had learned in our studies about living off the grid.

I'd also filled the wood bin to overflowing since I would be gone for a few days. Couldn't have my princess breaking a fingernail by having to haul in wood to stay warm.

There was no way in hell Addilyn would have let me go on my own, and keeping her locked up in the dead of winter for longer than a few hours wasn't possible.

But I could leave her without a vehicle, stranded until I returned.

I placed a note on the table, telling her I had things to take care of on my own that I didn't want her to have any part of and that I would be back in two days.

On March twelfth.

Her twenty-first birthday.

And I would come bearing gifts.

I retrieved a second throwaway phone I'd

hidden and placed it beside the note. It couldn't be traced, but if she had an emergency or if I didn't make it back to her, she would have a means of finding help.

Checking on her one last time showed she still lay like a corpse thanks to the crushed pill I'd slipped into her tea, unmoving except for the slight rise and fall of her chest.

I wanted to crawl back in bed with her. Hold her soft skin against mine, try to explain the feelings she brought to life inside me. Warmth and sunshine.

Not just obsession…*belonging*.

That I would go above and beyond to keep her safe, rage against anyone and anything if it meant staying by her side. My fucking princess—mine, goddamnit.

But duty called.

And I would erase every threat that stood in the way of our continued happiness.

Steeling myself, I turned and strode away. I had a two hour ride ahead of me.

And some sweet revenge to dish out.

***

I'd become one hell of a pill cocktail maker—and kidnapper. My adrenaline still pumped from nabbing my latest victim when I drove down into the seediest neighborhood in Anchorage. The one where the skanky cunts hung out hoping to swallow a guy's cum and make a few bucks.

The last known address of a girl I hadn't seen in a long fucking time, the stupid whore who didn't bother with privacy on social media and revealed to the world which street corner she used to pick up johns.

A lone streetlight flickered down the block, barely illuminating the dark, chilled night. Quiet settled over me where I sat in my car, the hum of the engine and heater enough to keep me company. I'd accomplished the first part of my plan for the night. Fingers crossed the second would arrive shortly.

Another twenty minutes passed before she hopped from a truck, waved to the guy, and sauntered up the sidewalk.

Free for the taking.

Adrenaline leaking into my bloodstream, I put the Subaru in drive and made my way toward her.

She sauntered, swaying a skinny ass tucked into tight jeans. A bulky jacket covered her upper body, but she turned as I slowed down alongside her, revealing a gaping zipper, her fake as fuck tits spilling out of a white tank top.

I crawled to a stop, putting the passenger window down, and I leaned to my right, tipping my baseball hat back so she'd see my face. "Jenny? Is that you?" I asked, forcing surprise into my voice and making my dimples pop.

She bent down, hands on the car, bloodshot eyes peering at me. Recognition lit, and she smiled, blinking lazily. "Gideon Destil. The fuck's a fine thing like you doin' down here?" she slurred. Probably high as a fucking kite, thank fuck.

"Just got out of jail. Hoping to find some action."

"Mmm." Her body weaved to the side like she could barely stand. "I could help you out." The flick of her tongue over her lower lip twisted my guts up tight as fuck.

I grinned anyway. "Hop in."

Jenny slid onto the passenger seat, filling my car with a waft of stale cigarettes, cheap perfume, and the musky scent of some guy's spunk.

She'd had a boob job. The fuckers heaved as she inhaled, sticking them out while settling into my car. I got caught staring, but I'd done it intentionally rather than throat punching the bitch like I'd have preferred to do.

"You're looking good, Jenny," I lied and licked my lower lip. "*Real* fucking good."

"Mmm." She leaned over and slid her hand up my thigh. "You too."

I grabbed her wrist tight enough to stop her from touching my limp dick but not harshly enough to hurt. "I spent years in prison fantasizing about having you under me."

She blinked, her skin pale, dark bags beneath her eyes. Her red lipstick was smeared like she'd had her mouth wrapped around the last guy to drop her off. "Get. Out." Fuck, even her breath smelled like cum.

My stomach considered heaving, but I brushed my thumb over her wrist, keeping my smile in place. "Seriously. I shouldn't have allowed myself to get distracted by my stepsister at Devon's party that night. I'd gone with one intention—and that was to finally give in to my lust for you."

She stared, mouth agape.

I held her gaze, allowing her to see heat in my eyes that didn't have a goddamn thing to do with her. "I always wanted you, Jenny. Tell me I can finally have you. Tell me I can steal you away to some hotel. Tie you up. Have my filthy way with you."

A soft gasp and the throb in her neck let me know she still hung onto that fantasy from when she and Addilyn had been younger and they couldn't get enough of Stolen, a Stockholm syndrome movie.

"Are you serious right now?" she breathed a vile exhale with the words, and I fought off a grimace.

"Dead." I held her stare, wondering how many Gideons she saw in her fucked-up vision. "You sober?"

She laughed, sitting back in the passenger seat, and I let go of her wrist. "Nope."

"You gonna remember the dick you fuck tonight with your tight cunt?"

Jenny squeezed her thighs together, shifting on the seat with a groan. "Fuck yeah."

"Good." I winked and drove away from the curb. "As long as you know who you're fucking, I can deal with a little buzzed beauty."

"You think I'm beautiful?" She slurred, settling her head against the rest behind her.

Fuck no.

"Always did, and with those tits?" I reached over and slid my hand into her shirt, grasping a handful of fake as fuck flesh. "Goddamn, woman."

She moaned like the whore she was while images of Addilyn flashed in front of my eyes.

My princess would claw my eyes out if she saw me feeling up the bitch who'd betrayed her...but Jenny needed to be all in for what I had planned.

"Where we goin'?" Jenny asked. "Tell me someplace close. Can't wait to finally have your cock, Gideon."

"I know, baby. I'm gonna give it to you too...so fucking hard." I pinched her nipple and pulled my hand away from her chest. The thought of what lay ahead of us through the overnight hours actually twitched my dick to life.

No blood had been spilled, but already the lust that came afterward from a bath of red crept through my veins.

I turned into a rundown motel, one I expected Jenny was well acquainted with. She still sat with her head tipped back, her gaze on me. I couldn't make out her eyes in the dark parking lot, but with the way she spoke and moved, I expected they'd be hazed over, pupils pinned.

Perfectly high like a soaring eagle.

"Here." I pulled two hundreds from my back pocket. "Go get us a room. Preferably the end one where it'll be quieter. Gonna make you scream so fucking hard, baby. Don't want to wake everyone up."

Jenny gulped and fumbled to grab my offering and open the car door.

"Hurry back," I murmured with a groan, pretending to adjust my blood lusting chub that wasn't yet strangled inside my jeans.

A stumble in her heels almost sent Jenny sprawling across the lot, but she shot out her hands, regaining her footing. The office door shut behind her, and I sat in silence once more, checking out the doors of the motel in front of me.

Three cars. One white, two darker in color.

Twelve fifty-five in the morning, I noted on the dashboard's clock.

Addilyn would have been awake for almost twenty-four hours. I wondered how many curses she'd sent my way. I wondered if she hated me for leaving her alone out there in the middle of nowhere. I wondered if she would accept and forgive me for the things I was about to do.

Jenny sauntered back toward my car, weaving like a drunken fool and spinning a keyring around her finger.

"Room on the end as requested," she stated all breathless while spilling back into my car.

"Good girl."

I backed into the last parking spot, thankful no streetlight shone to highlight my car. Trunk closest to the door—as needed. "Come on, baby," I said, yanking on my leather gloves and pushing open my car door. "Let's go get naked."

Jenny giggled and followed me.

A chuckle rumbled from my chest too.

She wouldn't be laughing if she knew what I had planned.

27

Gideon

I stayed behind, letting Jenny fumble with the key, my gaze sweeping left to right and back again beneath the ball cap I'd pulled down low on my brow. No one lingered outside from what I could see.

She finally got the door open, and I followed her in, taking care to not touch a goddamn thing. Before she could turn and jump on me, I grabbed her ass in a hard grip and shoved her forward a few stumbling steps. She caught herself on the edge of the bed, frowning at me.

I shot her a wink, slowly checking her out and sucking in my lower lip.

Her frown disappeared.

"Strip for me, baby," I murmured and sank into the chair beside the window with its closed blinds, my legs spread and gloved hands on my thighs.

"Give me a hot show, and I promise I'll make it good for you."

Jenny's pinned eyes heated, and she shrugged off her coat, letting it fall to the floor. An off-tune song hummed from her lips as she attempted a striptease, stumbling and giggling like a drunken fool. She managed to get her skintight jeans and panties off her legs without crashing to the floor.

I stopped her from dropping her tank top to the floor. "Blindfold yourself with it."

"Ooo," she moaned. "Kinky."

She had no fucking idea—but she was about to.

"I have this fantasy, Jenny."

"Do tell." She cupped her breast, but I held her hazed stare.

"You're the one who gave it to me actually." I cocked my head, smirking enough to show my dimples that used to gain me entry to whatever panties I wanted popped. "All those whispered conversations with my stepsister about being kidnapped, tied up…fuck, hearing you whimper about those things made *me* lust for them."

"Oh fuck."

"Yeah, baby…I want them. With you."

"I-I always thought you had a thing for Addilyn."

"Pfft." I snorted. "That goody-two-shoes? Please. Do you really believe she's the type of woman who would play the way I've wanted to?"

She let out a sarcastic laugh. "I see your point."

"But you…" I slid my gaze down over her gaunt body with the rounded tits. Bruised skin. Fucking needle tracks on her arms that made me want to puke. "You're the type of woman I've dreamed about. The kind of woman who would complete me."

"Gideon…" A shiver licked over her—probably partially from the fact the room was cold as fuck.

"Will you cover your eyes for me, baby? Let me have my wicked way with you—fulfill both our fantasies?"

The pulse thrummed in her neck, revealing what my words did to her.

Jenny, the stupid, trusting girl, obeyed.

And I fucking grinned, my adrenaline causing my dick to thicken.

"Christ, you're stunning," I groaned as though it was the sight of her affecting me and not the knowledge that my plan was working.

I stood and approached without quieting my footsteps, my lips curling as another tremor damn near sent her to her knees.

"Can you see me?" I murmured, inches from her body, ghosting my gloved fingertips over her covered eyes.

"No," she whispered with her foul breath.

Leaning toward her ear, I blew a hot exhale over her lobe. "I want to pretend that I didn't pick you up on the street corner, Jenny. Imagine I grabbed you instead. That you didn't come with me willingly—

that I had to hurt you, threaten you to keep you still and quiet in my car. Can you do that?"

She shivered again. "Uh huh."

"Pretend you're so damn scared, so damn turned on by being captured that you can't fight me. Shiver and shake for me, baby. Seeing your fear is going to make me so fucking hard—and we'll both enjoy the fuck out of tonight."

"God, Gideon." Jenny gulped, swaying on her feet.

"Can you do that for me? For us?"

"Yes." She jerked her head up and down. "Fuck, yes."

"On the bed," I ordered, the lowered rasp in my voice part of the playing—to hide my identity.

Just in case what I'd accomplished already for the night didn't work out as well as I had thought.

Jenny felt behind her for the edge of the mattress and did as told, propping up on her elbows to face me, legs spread in invitation.

"Gonna tie you up, baby." I gently grasped her ankle and spread her thighs wider. No footboard, but I'd considered the possibility and had brought along parachute cord from the cabin as well as the zip ties.

"Why are you still wearing your gloves?" Jenny pouted rather than growing nervous.

Stupid cunt.

"I'm playing my role. But tonight is all about

senses too. I'm going to touch you in so many hot as fuck ways that you're going to lose your voice from screaming my name."

"Oh God." She gulped as I looped the cord around her ankle.

At least the bed frame had legs so I didn't have to improvise too damn much. Four knots had her thighs spread wide, ankles tied down tight.

I trailed my gloved fingers up her outer leg, along her hip, over her navel, and between her breasts.

"The leather cool to the touch?" I asked, my voice rasped and tight as though turned on as fuck.

"Feels so fucking good." Jenny arched her back, and I gave one tit a firm squeeze to keep her arousal on edge.

"Fuck, Gideon," she groaned and shifted her hips. "Arms up."

She obeyed, and I strung the bitch up tight. Spread eagle. Like a goddamn feast to feed the blood rage I barely kept constrained.

I pulled my knife from the sheath at my waist and eyed the sharp as fuck blade. Considered slicing into her skin and slowly peeling it away from her body. But that would leave a bloody mess and cause the types of screams that would attract attention.

My dick twitched at the thought of hearing her cries for mercy I would never give, of soaking the mattress with her blood.

But I had something out in the car I needed

to get.

First things first…

I dragged the tip of my knife up the inside of her thigh, and she hissed, even though I didn't break skin. "The fuck is that?" She whimpered like a fearful little girl tied up for the big bad wolf.

"Knife," I replied casually, like I put on sneakers to head outside for a goddamn stroll.

She licked her lips and moaned. "The fuck you doin' with a knife?" Breathlessness let me know the horrible actress played along.

"I got this fetish…"

"You g-gonna cut me?" At least she added a stutter for effect. Not that it did a goddamn thing to my already thickened dick.

"Tell me how you're feeling," I ordered rather than answering.

Her hips shifted again like she tried to ease the ache between her thighs. "Fucking t-terrified."

"Mmm." She should be.

I spun the knife in my hand and slid the pommel up over her damp slit.

"Oh." Jenny lifted her hips. "You sick *fuck*."

"You have no idea," I rasped and rimmed her pussy with it, grimacing over the goddamn warts on her labia. "I'm going to fuck you with my knife."

"No." Jenny twisted like she tried to get away, but her lips smirked. "P-please don't touch me."

"I'm going do so much more than touch you."

I worked the pommel of my knife into her pussy a few inches, twisting it around.

"God…" Jenny lifted her hips, and I fucked into her a few times, keeping our little game going. The second I pulled the metal free from her body and set it aside, she whimpered.

Leaning down close to her face, I wafted my breath over her mouth as though about to kiss her. "Can you be a good little lamb and lay quiet for me, my sweet captive? I've got something out in the car I think you're going to like."

"Yeah. Oh, fuck yeah."

I left Jenny shivering on the bed and peeked through the room's curtains by the front door.

No one moved outside around the dark lot and the road beyond.

Adrenaline coursed through my blood as I opened the door and took the three steps to my trunk. The dark night sat quiet around us, my breath fogging in the cold air.

I wondered how my other friend fared.

Popping the trunk revealed he hadn't moved a goddamn muscle after those drugs, just like Twinkie's contact had promised. Blindfolded and with plugs shoved in his ears, even if he woke too early, he wouldn't be able to identify the one who'd stolen him from his house two hours earlier.

Let's go, lover boy.

Fucker wasn't light, and the only thing stiff about

him was the dick inside his lounge pants when I draped him over my shoulder in order to shut the trunk. Twinkie's man knew his shit when it came to Viagra and date rape cocktails. Chuckling, I brought my second guest into the motel room, locking us in for the next hour or so.

Jenny lifted her head off the pillow, head tracking as I moved along the edge of the room to the second bed beyond her. "Hold tight for me," I whispered with my growly tone—just in case the fucker on my shoulder could hear past the plugs.

"Hurry…I'm so damn wet for you."

Jaw clenched, I deposited my armload onto the empty bed, laying him out flat on his back like a damn corpse. The pulse beat in his neck—all the fuck I needed to know.

"You ready to make me a happy bastard?" I asked in my role's voice, yanking down Devon Bradshaw's lounge pants and revealing a straining, leaking dick.

"Fuck, yes," Jenny moaned.

Chuckling again, I returned to the whore, using my knife to cut her ankles free. I released one of her wrists, holding her left arm behind her back while doing the same with the other.

I lifted her onto her feet, keeping both of her arms behind her back. "I'm going to give you a dick to ride—and you'll use every goddamn trick in your little whore book to make him fill you up with his cum."

"G-Gideon…the fuck are you doing?"

Ignoring the stench of her skin and hair, I brushed my chest against her back, putting my face close to her ear. "Shh. Play with me, okay? I've got five years of fantasies locked up inside my head, Jenny. I need you to help me bring them to life."

"I gotta fuck another guy?"

Not just any guy…

"I want you to give me a little live porn with my buddy to get me ready for you, baby. Can you do that for this kinky fucker?"

"You're f-fucked up, Gideon."

"Yeah, and I think you love it. Now." I slipped a zip tie around her wrist when she didn't pull away or fight. "Show me if you're worthy of my dick, Jenny. Let me see what you've got, if that sweet pussy of yours is needy enough for *my* cum."

"Fuck." She shuddered, and I lifted her above the bed without even straining my arms. "Straddle him, baby. Let me put his dick inside you."

"Who is it?"

"Another captive." I chuckled—if only she knew. "You'll like his dick. It's got a thick head. Dripping," I whispered against her ear. "Gonna fill up your tight cunt. Get you sopping wet with his cum because you're going to need it to take my monster, baby."

"Oh fuck."

"Yeah. Now sit on his dick, Jenny."

28

Gideon

She spread her legs, kneeling atop our guest, and I grabbed hold of the leaking dick and positioned it against her diseased cunt.

"Ride him."

Jenny slammed herself onto Devon's dick without hesitation.

He didn't twitch. Didn't make a noise.

And I grinned like the sick fuck I was, stepping back to let the whore do her thing to a guy who wouldn't remember a second of what went down in the seedy hotel room where he would wake in the morning.

Jenny gasped and shifted her hips against Devon, riding him like a goddamn cowgirl hellbent on making him come, her arms tied behind her back.

"Yeah, baby," I groaned rather than gagging like I

wanted to. "You look like a fucking goddess…those gorgeous tits swaying. Fuck, my dick's like granite."

Wet sounds of fucking rose, adding to Jenny's moans and pants. Sweat broke out on her face, her thighs trembling from working so hard to please me.

"Fuuuuuuck, Jenny."

She whimpered.

"His balls are drawn up tight—he's gonna fucking bust a nut deep inside your cunt, baby," I rasped out and grunted like I grabbed my junk through my jeans. "Yeah. Keep going…just like that."

She rocked him so hard, the bed thumped against the outside wall.

I kept up with my spewed bullshit, praying Devon would be able to climax in his comatose, little blue-pill encouraged state. Part of the plan included proof of them having sex—

"Oh fuck!" Jenny shrieked. "He's coming…why isn't he making any noise?"

Sure enough, Devon's lower half involuntarily twitched beneath her, and she kept going, milking his balls. Desperate whore definitely wanted my dick.

She slowed, gasping for breath.

I lifted her by her arms, and she half-stumbled over to the other bed where I set her down.

"You did so good. Christ, what a show." I smoothed her arms a bit and cut the zip ties free.

"But now it's our turn. Lay back for me, Jenny. Let me have my way with you."

Still sucking in oxygen, she did as told, and I retied her arms to the headboard.

She rubbed her hips on the mattress, chasing what she expected to get, something she would never have from me even if my cock did throb inside my jeans.

"Naughty little captive." I made a tsking noise, running my gloved hand down her thigh. "Guess I'm going to have to tie you up tight, huh?"

She moaned her agreement, and I bit my tongue to keep from laughing.

Once more spread eagle, unable to move, Jenny lay waiting.

For my revenge.

Grimacing, I picked up her panties off the floor. Kinkier and more in line for the scene than say a towel from the bathroom.

"Going to gag my pretty captive," I told Jenny, readying a piece of rope to tie it in place.

"What?"

"Can't have you screaming my name too loud and waking the neighbors," I whispered, gently prying her lips open. "Let me put this in your mouth, and when we're done, maybe I'll give you something more against your tongue."

She dropped open her jaw like she was hungry for it.

"That's my sweet girl," I cooed, gently putting her balled up panties in her mouth. "Okay?"

"Mmm." She nodded and shifted.

I wrapped the cord around her head, tight enough to keep the gag in place, and stepped back to eye the two fuckers in the hotel room with me. One panting and trembling for dick, the other's shaft glistening and limp between his lax thighs.

Both at my mercy.

I hefted Devon into my arms and carried him over to Jenny's bed.

She jerked on the mattress as I sprawled Devon's dead weight atop her, muffled noises escaping around her gag. Thrashing, she tried to holler while I arranged his body between her thighs, his chest against her belly.

I climbed atop them on my knees, lifting Devon's hands in my gloved ones to Jenny's neck.

She stilled and garbled an inquiry I couldn't make out.

"This is for Addilyn," I growled, "you disloyal *cunt.*"

I squeezed Devon's hands around Jenny's neck, cutting off her oxygen.

Jenny tried to thrash beneath our combined weight, tried to jerk her head from his grasp I forced without his knowledge.

Muffled shrieks tightened my groin. Gasps and gurgles fed the bloodlust raging in my gut.

Revenge at its sickest, its sweetest.

She stilled far sooner than I expected, but I didn't remove Devon's hands, counting my heartbeats thumping in ears for a full two minutes.

Realizing I heaved for breath, I released my hold on Devon.

His hands slid to the side of Jenny's neck. Limp.

The pulse in his neck beat at a steady pace, but Jenny's didn't.

Adrenaline coursed through me as I climbed off the bed and took in my work.

One dead, the other ruined for life.

Three in the morning—the clock on the bedstand blinked.

I retrieved the blindfold from Devon and did one last sweep of the hotel room to make sure I hadn't left anything that would bring attention to a third party having been involved in their tryst.

After a good thirty seconds' worth of peering across the empty parking lot, I took the final evidence—the ear plugs from Devon's ears.

Quiet as a goddamn mouse, I slipped out of the room and escaped into the night, my adrenaline still pumping.

Still far from satisfied.

29

Addilyn

My body weighed into the mattress, heavy and exhausted. Warmth surrounded me, and I stretched like a leisurely cat, wincing at the soreness riddling my body.

Gideon had held me face down on the bed, arms wrapped behind my back while he'd fucked first my pussy then my ass, using only my own arousal as lubricant.

My backside ached like he'd ripped me a new hole back there, but the tea he'd made had helped me rest regardless of the stinging that refused to relent.

Blinking, I brought the dim bedroom into focus. Light filtered through the open doorway and the windows beyond. While comfortable beneath the quilt, coolness kissed over my face.

I sat, wrapped the blanket around my nakedness,

and got up to patter across the cold floorboards, wondering at the strangeness hazing my head that I couldn't blink away. Felt a little bit too familiar, but Gideon wouldn't have a reason to drug me again.

He wasn't in the living area, and the opened bathroom door revealed he wasn't in there either.

"Gideon?" I croaked and cleared my throat, glancing around the room. Why did I still feel half dead if I'd slept the night away? Mere embers lay in the fireplace, and alongside, the wood stack overflowed its bin.

He never left the fire unattended.

My heart picked up a bit, and I hurried to the window beside the front door, the weakness in my legs causing me to stumble twice. I clutched the window frame with one hand to keep upright, blinking to focus on the landscape through the glass.

No car.

No Gideon.

He left me.

Throat tight, I stared across the frozen land, at the tracks leading away through the trees toward the main road. He'd abandoned me out in the middle of the wilderness.

My stomach roiled, and I swallowed rising bile. Head fuzzy. Body achy…

He *had* drugged me again…the jackass fucking drugged me!

Spinning, I breathed hard through my nose to

keep from spewing, clutching the blanket around me.

Gideon Destil had finally gotten me to ride his dick like he'd talked about while we were teens, he'd tasted my ass—he'd taken his revenge on me.

I melted to the floor, fighting against the sobs wanting to rip from my chest. Never had I felt more broken or hollower. As though the world pressed down on my shoulders, I sank sideways, curled up in a ball. Eyes wide and staring at the cold fireplace.

Alone…

Or had he left me for Lloyd's taking?

A shiver slid up my spine, raising the hairs on my nape.

I need to get out of here.

But my heart sat heavy in my chest, weighing me down. I couldn't move. Didn't want to. His departure fractured the deepest parts of me, and even though my mind screamed for me to get dressed and get the fuck down the road toward civilization, my body refused to rouse from its stupor.

Let Lloyd show up. Let him have his way with me.

Living without Gideon wouldn't be worth the effort. What did I care if Lloyd ended up with Mother's money, my inheritance? What was having the means to live comfortably worth if I couldn't do it with my other half beside me?

Tears slid down my face, and I didn't bother

stopping them. Gideon *was* my other half. He understood me, gave me what I needed to feel alive. Made me think that perhaps I wasn't so sick after all.

How could he not feel the same? How could he deny the bond between us, drug me a second time, and simply take off?

Why hadn't he laughed in my face? Soaked in my horror as I learned the truth of his revenge against me?

It didn't make sense.

But neither did the lack of expression on his face over watching Devon's father being led from his house in handcuffs.

Didn't he experience emotion beyond anger and lust? Was he incapable of anything more? Having Lloyd as a father, he could certainly be broken, but I thought he had let me in.

He'd asked me to trust him in the car the day before. Maybe he really did have something planned he couldn't share with me.

Grabbing hold of the thought and clinging tight, I pushed up to sit, slouched and shivering in the cold.

Fire.

I needed heat or I would freeze to death in the Alaskan wilderness. Gideon would hate me if he'd been telling the truth and I'd been too burdened by hurt and depression to survive until his return.

Wiping my wet cheeks on the blanket, I half-crawled to the fireplace, grasping that tiny spark of hope in my chest.

A few glowing chunks of burned-down wood remained, flaring to life a little as I used the poker to stir them. I grabbed a few pieces of kindling from the bucket, laid them atop, and gently blew on the base as I'd seen Gideon do every morning before we'd gone to Anchorage.

Glowing red embers soon caught into flame, tiny flickers of yellow and orange crackling at the small pieces of wood. Warmth caressed my face, and I huddled close, soaking in the comfort of not feeling so alone.

The heat grew, and I stacked a couple split logs atop.

Flames licked higher, and I stared from a greater distance, still trying to wake fully from the drugs. Still shivering.

Why had he drugged me?

I frowned, puzzling on why he'd do such a thing. Had he known I would argue at being left behind? Did he go somewhere dangerous, some place he might get caught and was trying to keep me from harm?

My heart clung to that thought, telling myself my protector would do nothing less.

Clutching my quilt tight, I turned toward the kitchen area and headed for the one thing that would wake me up.

Coffee. I needed a clearer mind. Needed to put pieces of truth together in my head—

A piece of paper and cell phone sat on the table.

I leaped forward on weak legs, swiping the paper up.

Gideon had something to take care of on his own that he didn't want me to have any part of. He'd be home in a couple days…on my twenty-first birthday, and he would come bearing gifts.

My legs gave out again, and I sank to the floor for a second time, clutching the paper to my bare chest. Tears once more rolled as relief left me shaky and grinning like an idiot.

He hadn't left me.

He'd protected me the only way he knew how, hiding me away where no one would find me.

Gideon hadn't lied—even if he did knock me out with a drugged tea, the jackass.

I sniffed, wiped my tears, and let out a shaky laugh.

He would return to me on my birthday once it was too late for Lloyd to hurt me.

If he'd explained what he planned, I wouldn't have argued. I'd have sat in the cozy cabin as the hours slipped past, waiting for my birthday, for the day I could legally claim what belonged to me— leaving Lloyd with nothing.

March twelfth, my birthday, arrived, and I sat on the couch, warm from the fire and the cell in my hand.

Waiting.

Growing anxious.

The afternoon went on too long.

And Gideon never called like I had hoped and expected him to. Why leave me a cell otherwise?

I didn't have the number to his phone, and the only one I knew by heart besides 911 was Ciarra's.

Chewing my fingernails to the quick didn't help pass time any faster or ease the tightness in my stomach.

Had something happened to Gideon? Had whatever plans he'd made gotten him arrested again? Was I sitting and twiddling my thumbs…for nothing?

Hands shaking, I dialed Ciarra.

She didn't answer, but she rarely did if it was a caller whose number she didn't recognize.

I called again.

A third time.

"Come on…"

The fourth time, I sat biting my lip, eyes closed, begging her to pick up.

Please…please…

"Hello?" She snapped, and the air left my lungs in a rush.

"Ciarra!"

"Addilyn? What the hell? Where are you? I've

been desperate to get ahold of you. Holy hell, woman!"

"I'm fine…everything's good." My voice shook, and I laughed over the tension releasing in my stomach.

"Tell me you didn't have anything to do with this, Addilyn. Seriously. It's fucked up. Shit like this doesn't happen around here!"

Anxiety clenched my insides again. "What are you talking about?"

"The news! It's all over every major headline, on every station."

"What happened?"

"Devon. He strangled Jenny. Says he doesn't remember doing it…"

Ciarra went on and on while I stared at the fire, processing the only lines I'd heard from her mouth.

Devon strangled Jenny.

He didn't remember doing it.

Gideon.

I swallowed hard, my eyes stinging.

We hadn't made any plans for revenge for either of them. He'd set something in place for the sheriff and his father. That was it.

If anyone wanted revenge on Jenny, it would have been me…I was the one she'd betrayed by sharing the story I'd told her about the night after Gideon had beat Devon to a bloody pulp.

"Jesus," I whispered past the nausea in my belly, my response shutting Ciarra up.

"Where are you? Tell me you're innocent in all this."

"I am. Swear to God," I managed to croak out. "I-I'm not anywhere near Anchorage."

But Gideon doubtless was. "What happened again?" I asked, hoping my cringe didn't come through in my voice.

Ciarra repeated what she'd already spewed, telling me about the run-down motel where the owner had found Devon passed out on top of Jenny. She'd been tied up. Gagged and blindfolded.

Both of them naked with evidence of a fuckfest Devon Bradshaw wouldn't ever be able to deny, no matter how much he screamed about his innocence while being dragged away in handcuffs from the scene.

One newscaster even got his fiancée on video, splotchy-faced from crying, stating about Jenny being Devon's ex-girlfriend who she'd had to get a restraining order against.

She didn't understand. Was heartbroken.

"Is Gideon with you?" Ciarra asked.

"Yes," I didn't hesitate to lie to my best friend, even though doing so turned my insides out.

I'd been burned once before by the very whore who never woke up from her night with Devon—and probably Gideon if I had to guess.

I couldn't trust someone with the truth in such a way ever again. Doing so put more than my own well-being in danger.

She let out a heavy breath. "Seriously, this is fucked up."

"You're telling me."

Twenty minutes later, after assuring Ciarra for the third time that I was fine, I hung up and sat in stifling silence.

I imagined the scene the motel owner must have walked in on. The crack whore cold and stiff beneath an upstanding young man who'd had the world in front of him.

Her dead.

Him ruined.

Justice as far as I was concerned, and not one lick of remorse or regret whispered through my conscience.

If Gideon had been the one responsible, I expected he would have been riding that blood rage since the night before. Believing he'd given me my gift, I banked the fire and readied for bed.

He would be home before long and need me to sate the lust I didn't doubt held his full focus.

My core warming, I crawled into our bed and waited for his return.

30

Gideon

I knew I shouldn't stick around but couldn't help myself. The need to enjoy the consequences of my actions play out made me park two blocks away from the motel.

The owner meandered down the sidewalk two hours after checkout time to see why the room on the end hadn't emptied. He found it full—and sprinted back toward the office, his fat gut bouncing with every step.

Adrenaline had its way with me, but I sat still, loving the sound of sirens and the sight of flashing lights minutes later.

Devon appeared in the doorway, naked, breath puffing white with every panted exhale.

Guns were drawn, trained on him as he stumbled from the room, hands held high.

I cracked my window so I could hear.

"I didn't do it!" He shrieked like a little girl while being slammed onto the ground.

Smelling of Jenny's dirty cunt. Hopefully, his dick crushed into pavement as diseased as she'd been. Tossed into the back of a squad car like I'd been, shoulders hunched.

Defeated.

The fuckface had gotten what was coming to him.

I started my car and eased away from the scene, my heart racing, grinning like a madman.

One man remained on my radar, but not for long. Best to get ahold of him before he saw the news and grew suspicious.

I called the fucker who'd spawned me, only the excitement to finish things keeping me awake.

"Clear your schedule for the rest of the day," I said when Lloyd answered.

"It's her fucking birthday," he screamed over the line, and my grin widened.

"And I broke her good. She's all ready and waiting for you, Dad." I tossed in the title I hadn't used for him in my head for over five years.

"I've got a meeting I can't miss this afternoon. Where is she?" he snipped, revealing his anxiety.

"Some place you'll never find on your own." I gave him the coordinates of where he needed to meet me so I could take him to her. "The cabin is off the grid, and the driveway is hard to navigate. We can drive out there together and end this shit once and for all."

He agreed, so damn on edge and desperate for my princess that he didn't act the least bit suspicious.

Dumb fucker.

A few hours later, I arrived at our meeting point in middle of nowhere, a simple gravel parking area I'd found weeks earlier when I'd decided on Lloyd's fate. With it being off the beaten path, I didn't fear sitting there to wait.

It would be days, maybe even weeks, before his car was found.

Empty.

No trace of where he'd gone and no tire tracks from my car in the snow thanks to the warming weather promised by forecasters for the next couple of days.

I snacked on the granola bars and apples I'd brought from the cabin since the sandwiches I'd packed were long gone, and I laid back my seat, forcing my eyelids shut. Strength would be needed for what lay ahead, and I couldn't fuck up now that I was so damn close to finishing.

The flash of headlights had me sitting upright. Dad's SUV, the one he'd given me a ride in when I'd gotten out of jail, pulled in alongside me.

He shut off his vehicle and climbed out, the chirp of the lock telling me he wouldn't question my suggestion to drive him to the cabin.

And that he either hadn't heard about Devon and Jenny's demise or was too stupid to be suspicious.

Dark clothes, not the office type, suggested he knew what lay ahead…or rather, what he thought he had planned.

Blood.

While true, it wouldn't be anyone's but his shed tonight.

"How far?" He grunted while buckling himself into my passenger seat.

I started up the cold car and eased out onto the road before answering. "Hour, give or take."

"Where the hell are we going?"

Somewhere they'll never find your body.

"Old cabin northwest of here," I replied rather than voicing what went through my mind. "Belongs to a guy I knew in jail."

"The bitch is still alive?"

"For now."

"Did you hurt her good?"

I relived a few moments of breaking her in my mind, her back slammed against the wall while I fucked her pussy. Her ass stretched around my dick and the tears she'd cried. "Yeah," I fought to keep a lustful rasp from my voice.

Lloyd grunted his acknowledgement.

But I wanted more than that. I wanted to hear from his own lips how he'd defiled my princess. I wanted him to admit to raping his stepdaughter.

"But probably not as much as you're going to." I kept my tone conversational.

Lloyd's snicker flared the blood rage back to life in my gut.

"She's a kinky slut. Never got off unless I inflicted pain in some way."

My jaw ached from clenching my teeth.

"She too far gone for one last fuck?"

I shook my head—but it wouldn't be him doing the fucking. "She's waiting for you." I wasn't so sure about that, but I hoped like fuck she was.

"I'm proud of you, son."

I glanced at him, my lips tight. Out of all the times I'd longed to hear those words from his mouth, I sure as fuck hadn't expected them for kidnapping a woman, breaking her, and giving him the chance to hurt her.

Fucker. He gazed at me with softness in his eyes as though he really meant it while I fought to control the beast wanting to rip his face off.

"Been wanting to hear you say that to me for a long time."

Lloyd clasped my shoulder. "It's nice to find my son has grown into a real man. We've got one hell of a future ahead of us. I'm going to put you on my company's board once we take care of this last bit keeping us from claiming my money."

His company, his money.

I wanted to snort. Wanted to plant my fist in his

motherfucking mouth to shut him the hell up. I wanted to slice off his dick and shove it so far down his throat he gagged on his own flesh, same as he'd made Addilyn do.

Maybe I'd fuck him with a hot poker, bleed his ass out. Stab into his prostate and fuck him there, to burn his insides like he'd done to my princess.

"What's my cut of that money?" I asked instead, adding a gleam to my eyes while turning forward again in case he attempted to read my face.

"Twenty-five percent."

I nodded rather than arguing. No sense in pissing him off or putting him on edge. "Since you're offering me a job, I guess that means I'm coming back to Ingrid's house once we're done with this shit?"

"My house," he stated as though the deed was already done. "And if you do want to move in until you find something else, I can have the housekeeper ready your old room."

"Let's take care of the backstabbing bitch first," I said, grinning at the thought of what emotions would cross Addilyn's face when I gave her the birthday gift I'd promised. "Then we can go home and toast to our good fortune with that scotch shit you used to love so much."

No lights shone from the cabin when I approached even though the dashboard clock showed five minutes to ten. Flicking off the headlights, I crept forward to park, hoping I wouldn't wake my sleeping beauty—if she slept.

"You left her in the dark?" Lloyd asked with a chuckle.

"It's one of the things she fears the most," I mumbled, turning off the car. "Besides you."

"Let's go bring her nightmares to life."

Pretending to conspire with Lloyd roiled my guts, and I had to force the smile that mirrored his as we climbed out.

Taking my time shutting my car door put him ahead of me in walking to the cabin's door—right the fuck where I wanted him. Adrenaline rushed through my body, warming my extremities, and the promise of blood got my dick twitching to life. Retrieving my knife from its sheath, I stepped closer.

Pulse thrumming.

Hands steady.

The fucker was so intent on getting to Addilyn that he hadn't considered I might double cross him.

My grin returned, my dick hardening like stone.

Stupid fuck.

One swing of my fist planted the pommel against his temple. Lloyd crumpled to the ground.

My blood rushed through my arteries, my heart rate pulsing to the point I panted. A quick glance at the cabin's dark windows let me know we hadn't woken Addilyn.

Or had she taken off on foot after waking and realizing I'd drugged her?

"Fuck."

My dick had swelled fully, thinking it would soon find release inside her body, but what if she didn't lay there in wait?

I glanced down at Lloyd. Flicked my gaze to the cabin.

Couldn't leave the fucker outside alone for even two minutes in case he came to.

Teeth clenched, I set aside my desire to know the whereabouts of my princess, and I dragged Lloyd to the woodshed where a chair and parachute cord sat ready.

He carried his wallet and cell phone in his pockets, the latter of which I dismantled and crushed beneath my heel.

His dead weight made for an awkward haul in getting him upright, but within ten minutes, I had the fucker bound with his arms behind his back and his ankles tight to the chair's front legs—which I'd bolted to the plank floor.

No chance in hell he'd be able to wobble over, crash, and break the chair beneath him.

My fucking father's fate had been sealed.

While I'd have loved to sit and wait for him to wake and come to the realization *I* was the backstabber, the need to make sure Addilyn hadn't left me in a fit of rage decided my steps.

Anxiety, the possibility of warm, wet flesh, grasping hands, and the only place I wanted to find release from the bloodlust inside me brought me back outside.

I locked the woodshed behind me.

Pulse still thrumming, my dick hard as fuck, I let myself into the cabin.

From the doorway, I could make out the lump on the bed beyond the kitchen area.

An unsteady exhale emptied my lungs, and I kicked off my boots rather than stomping her way and waking her. In socked feet, I crept across the cabin and into the bedroom.

My Addilyn lay curled on the bed, lips parted in sleep. The oil lamp was turned low on the bedstand I'd put back into the room after her captivity had ended.

Sleeping peacefully, she had no fucking clue the state of my mind or my leaking dick.

But that was all about to change.

31

Addilyn

Gideon's energy radiated over my body, rousing me awake—and his grasp on my thighs as he yanked me close had me opening my eyes. One vicious rip snatched my panties clear off my body, my thighs stinging from the abrasion of cotton.

"Gide—" His name tore from my lips with a gasp as he shoved his face between my thighs, tongue going straight into my pussy. "Oh…oh God…"

Fingers tugging at his head, I held him close while he ate me out, his groans and grunts bringing on a rush of arousal he lapped up like a starving man.

I couldn't think, couldn't breathe. A whimpered exhale from my lips seemed to feed his hunger.

"Ten times better than your panties," he growled and dove back in.

I wrapped my legs around his shoulders, smiling over memories of finding him jerking off with my panties.

"Fuck, princess." He backed away and smacked my clit, sending a jolt clear through to my spine.

Shrieking, I tried to scoot away, but he held me firm on one thigh, his fingertips bruising. He leaned in, sucking on my clit hard enough I winced. Teeth scraping. Tongue soothing.

"Gideon," I moaned, hungering for more.

He shoved two fingers into my core, curled them, and rubbed at my g-spot. Hard.

"Oh shit!" I shrieked as he enticed my body to squirt all over his hand.

"Fuck, yeah…so fucking sexy. Need this pussy. So damn bad."

"Take it," I gasped, lifting my hips to force his fingers deeper, desperate for the intimacy between us.

"Fuck." He hopped from the bed, ripped off his clothes, and climbed back toward me, his eyes dark, feral in the soft lamplight on the bedstand.

My heart raced, and my lips parted as I held his stare.

Standing on the mattress, he wrapped his hands beneath my ass and lifted me high, nearly bending me in half. "Take a deep breath, princess," he warned, his tone gravelly, sexy as hell.

Squatting, he shoved his dick down into my

pussy with one grunted thrust before my lungs filled.

"Oh fuck!" I pressed my neck back, teeth clenched against the burn, his length almost too much to bear.

"Fuck." The cords in his neck stood out, and a dozen more curses spilled from his lips. "So goddamn tight. Jesus."

I damn near choked over how he held me bent. "So deep—this—way," I gasped out as he drilled into me, his thighs bunching, muscles straining.

The black of his pupils ate up the blue, like a devil focused on claiming my soul. "Take it. All of it."

"Yes—yes, Gideon—give it to me."

With our gazes locked, he fucked me hard and fast, animalistic grunts ripping from his lips that took my arousal to a higher level. Wetness smeared between us, the sounds of our fucking filthy as fuck.

"Needed you." Gideon lowered my body to the mattress, keeping us connected, his hips thrusting without pause. He covered me with damp skin and hard muscle, his mouth finding my neck.

I grabbed hold of his back, fingernails digging in along his spine, the energy between us lighting up my skin like a live wire.

His teeth bruised, but I loved the pulse beneath his mouth and the way it pumped pure euphoria through my body. I lusted for more. The pain. The pleasure. I wanted his marks on my skin, to be claimed with sweat. Blood. Claimed with his cum.

"My sweet release," he murmured against my neck as he rotated his hips, his pelvis rubbing my clit.

"G-gonna come."

"Yeah…soak my dick, princess." He planked while fucking into me, watching my face. "Come all over me."

I did—a gush of cum while I shrieked his name.

"Jesus…fuck…" He clenched his jaw, lips thinning and nostrils flaring to suck in oxygen.

My thoughts scattered as Gideon pounded into me, drawing out my climax. He took me to a place where darkness, sickness didn't exist—a place more addictive than any drug.

I dug my fingernails into his back deep enough to draw blood, but I couldn't bring him closer. Deeper. So damn burrowed inside me he wouldn't know our souls apart.

Vicious thrusts accompanied his grunts. Grinding as though he hoped to gain another inch inside my throbbing core.

"Yes." He groaned, and his release against my womb sent another climax rushing through me.

"Why did you leave me?" I asked quietly.

His eyes remained open, vulnerable. "I had shit to take care of I didn't want you having any part in. Just like I stated in my note."

"Did it have anything to do with what happened to Devon and Jenny?"

He stilled from rubbing my back in slow circles. "How did you see the news?"

"I didn't. I called Ciarra this afternoon when I couldn't handle waiting to hear from you any longer."

His thumb took back up its circling motion. "What'd she tell you?"

"That Devon killed Jenny. Choked her out."

Gideon slid his hand up to my neck, a single fingertip tracing what was probably bruising on my skin.

"You did it, didn't you?" I whispered.

"They hurt my princess." A nonchalant statement, not a direct answer, but I didn't need one.

I leaned forward and brushed my lips over his, letting him know without words that he had my thanks, that whatever horror he'd unleashed on both of my old friends would never change the way I felt about him.

He'd framed Devon. Killed my old best friend, and I couldn't find a single fuck to give. I hoped she'd suffered. I hoped Devon rotted in prison. Gideon had a screw loose in his head, one born of anger that reveled in violence, but the secret part of his soul only made me want him more.

Sick, but what we shared, the beautiful connection between us, was above ethics. Moral codes didn't matter when it came to us.

Exhaustion and contentment swept through me, and I rested on the pillow we shared, our gazes locked.

I accepted Gideon for who he was, broken pieces and all—because he did the same for me. Always had. It was like we were two puzzle pieces that fit together in all ways. A perfect match.

In that moment, I realized I *had* found my other half, truly and surely—and that was who I was meant to be.

His.

My throat tightened, and emotions rose to my lips, three words I wanted to tell him—

"I have a present for you."

Even though I was tired and had lost the chance to explain how I felt, I smiled over the fact he'd remembered a gift for my birthday. "What is it?"

"It's in the woodshed."

My brow furrowed in a slight frown. "What?"

"Your gift." He kissed my nose and rolled from the bed, leaving me chilly. "Come on."

Well, okay then.

He pulled on his clothes, and I did the same,

eyeing him. A glint had returned to his eyes and a curl to his lips.

Whatever he'd brought me made him giddy. Excited.

My belly fed off his vibes, and I tugged on my coat, ready to follow him out into the dark.

He held a flashlight in one hand and grasped mine in his other.

Cold bit at my face, and my breath puffed, but warmth filled me through. What the hell had he lugged back from Anchorage that couldn't be inside the house?

A pet of some sort? Why not just take it to the house? And why a pet anyway? I'd never wanted one or mentioned such a thing.

Clueless, I frowned again as he let go of my hand to unlock the wooden door. He swung it open and flicked on the light.

His broad back kept me from seeing what he'd brought—but he stepped off to the side.

My breath snagged.

Lloyd.

Tied to a chair.

Blood dripping down over his temple.

Dark eyes piercing mine.

"Happy birthday, princess," Gideon murmured against my ear, causing my hairs to stand on end.

32

Gideon

ddilyn blinked. Stared from the shed's doorway.

"The fuck is this?" Lloyd cursed, yanking on the binds he'd never be able to break.

"It's called revenge, asshole." I shot him a glare, my desire for blood rousing again. "You really think I would give up the most precious thing in my life to you? Are you really that fucking stupid to believe I don't know when you're lying? You uncovered my juvie records, Lloyd. Without those, I never would've been convicted."

"It was her words that got you locked up."

The fuckface didn't argue the truth I'd stated.

"My princess was an innocent," I said, the growing rage in my gut wanting to unleash. Stalking forward, I held his gaze and fed off the fear budding in his eyes. "*Was,*" I repeated with emphasis, "until you helped send me away so you could steal that innocence from her."

My fist shot out without thought, smashing into his cheek.

Blood sprayed across the floor, but it was his grunt and Addilyn's gasp that fed my bloodlust. Rage no longer simmered—it flared to life.

I turned to find her watching me heave for breath, my hands fisted at my sides.

No fucking trace of horror or disgust shone in her wide blue eyes.

My strong princess…fuck did she know how to light up my insides.

"I'm going to make him pay for what he did to you, Addilyn," I promised with a harsh, guttural tone. "He's going to hurt like you did. Beg for mercy."

"But you won't give it," she whispered.

I grinned at her statement, how she was unaffected by what I had planned. "Fuck no."

Lips pressing in a tight line, she turned to watch Lloyd bleed. "Good."

"You make me hard as hell, Addilyn Jane Reed." Without waiting for a response to what she already knew to be true, I shifted my focus back on Lloyd. "Sick fucks like you don't deserve to live."

Lloyd spat out blood, still having the balls to glare at me. "She's only using you, son."

"I'm not your son," I hollered, my short finger-nails digging into my palms.

"She'll get what she wants from you then leave you hanging, desperate for more like she did with me."

"I never wanted you!" Addilyn shrieked from behind me. "You lying fuck!"

"She was a cock hungry little girl," Lloyd continued, ignoring her and holding my stare, "lusting to fulfill all the fantasies she cooked up in her head because of the porn she'd been watching."

"Liar!" she screamed, her anger, her pain feeding the beast inside me.

"Every day she pleaded for my dick." Lloyd sneered. "To give her the kind of pain that she craved."

My gut simmered as I listened to his lies, but I needed him to keep on…giving me a reason to bleed him out. To watch the life fade from his eyes after the hours of torture he fucking deserved.

"She. Got. Off." Lloyd bit out each word with a sick smirk on his mouth. "Begged for me to take her ass. Got on her knees, asking me to fuck her face with my dick."

Addilyn choked on a sob but didn't refute his claims.

"She wanted my dick every day," Lloyd continued. "Cried whenever she got her period and I denied her."

Still Addilyn stood silent behind me.

"And when she found out that last time I'd emptied my balls inside her mother rather than her needy little cunt?" Lloyd snorted, shaking his head. "My wife needed surgery to repair the scars on her cheek from Addilyn's fingernails."

I couldn't bear to take my focus off of Lloyd as a slither of doubt crept into my mind. All the shit he stated, she hadn't mentioned, and it seemed too detailed to be lies conjured up out of desperation.

Had I misplaced my loyalty?

My guts clenched into a knot, and I considered filleting him open in order to read him like a book.

Lloyd had managed to manipulate me into believing him once before, but I'd been high on emotion and anger, unwilling to differentiate between the lies he'd told and the truth. I studied his face, but he continued spewing shit before I could make up my mind.

"I can't tell you how many times her pussy tried to suck my balls dry, Gideon. Crying out her release, her cum creaming my dick. I fulfilled every single one of her fantasies. Tied up. Choked out. Marked with my cum."

Everything I did to her—

"No," Addilyn finally voiced denial, her tone weak—but firm. "You...you sick fuck! I never wanted your touch. Your dick. Your mouth on me!"

"Who's the sick fuck?" Lloyd asked, eyeing her.

"You're nothing more than a piece of trash. A kinky whore who wanted her stepfather's dick."

My princess...the only one who understood and accepted me for the sick fuck *I* was. And Lloyd thought to liken her to the bitch I'd helped Devon strangle?

The rage exploded, and my fist shot out again, smashing into his mouth and knocking his head back.

He let out a grunt. Groaned while spitting out a tooth. "Fuck." He spat again, blinking and muttering curses.

"She's fucking perfect," I growled at him, the adrenaline keeping my fists numb to the pain from thrashing at him. "Don't ever compare her to someone like that junkie Jenny!"

Lloyd's eyes widened as I yanked my knife from its sheath and closed the distance between us. "Th-that was you?"

"Fuck yeah," I answered, my lips twitching upward in a manic grin. "So was getting your friend hauled off in cuffs." I pressed my blade against Lloyd's neck, causing his movements to still.

His gaze flicked beyond me, fear returning to his dark orbs. The kind that twitched my dick to life. The kind I fed off.

"Tell me why I shouldn't slice every inch of you into ribbons. Soak the floor with your blood." I leaned down, putting our faces at eye level. "Because that's what I want, Lloyd. I want your pain. Your screams. I want to take back everything you *stole* from my princess."

A shudder rippled through me at the images flashing in my head.

Devon and Jenny had been a quiet affair.

The Sheriff's even more so since I hadn't gotten my hands dirtied.

But this...the start of it all, will give me the bloodbath I need.

My grin widened.

"Don't do this, son."

I stabbed the knife into his clavicle, and his scream filled the night. Closing my eyes, I soaked that shit up.

Chuckled.

"Jesus—fuck!" Lloyd gasped, and I yanked the blade out.

"I'm not your fucking *son*." I stabbed into his other shoulder, his shrieks a growing crescendo in my ears.

Addilyn didn't ask me to stop. Didn't make one goddamn noise of disgust over the violent streak rising to claim my mind.

I sliced Lloyd's shirt from his body. Yanked the blood-soaked cotton free. Let it fall with a wet splat to the floor.

"Gideon..." he tried to sway me, but the simple

pleading of my name on his bloody lips made no difference.

Addilyn deserved her revenge, and I would be the one to give it to her.

Shoving the knife's tip into his pec, I watched Lloyd's eyes as he hissed. He blinked while I dragged the blade across his chest.

"Fuck!" He tipped his head back, a ribbon of red trickling down over his stomach. "Goddamnit, Gideon...please. Please don't do this."

I stabbed lower and created another gash.

No sound from Addilyn—but the fuckface bleeding red for me cried out.

Not nearly loud enough.

Smirking, I twirled the knife's pommel in my hand.

"Gid—"

I buried the fucking blade in his thigh, cutting off his pleading.

He screamed like a goddamn woman, tone high pitched and fucking luscious.

My dick swelled, and like the sick fuck I was, I gave him a matching stab wound on the opposite thigh.

"Stop!" He screamed, trying to buck in his bindings. "Please. Fucking Christ, Gideon! Please!"

"How many times did she beg the same from you?" I stabbed through his kneecap.

Bloody fucking screams... Jesus...

"Huh? How many fucking times, Lloyd?" I buried the blade in his other knee and twisted the thing the best I could, drawing out his shrieks. Sucking the scents of coppery blood and his fear deep into my lungs. Fucking getting off on how he attempted to escape the chair of death.

Powerless.

Same as my princess had been.

I sliced off his pants, his boxers. Left him sitting naked in the cold, covered in blood.

My breath puffed in front of my face as I panted, watching him wilt. Shudder.

"You're a covetous bastard, and you deserve to rot in hell," I told him, knife tip touching his nose and lifting his head.

His dark eyes glazed by pain held no trace of hope.

And I fed off that shit, my body buzzing.

He'd manipulated me—and Addilyn—and karma was about to make him her bitch.

"I'm going to peel the skin off your body, Lloyd, an inch for every time you fucked what didn't belong to you."

Grinning, I stepped forward and began fulfilling my promise.

33

Addilyn

Numbness held me in place—like I watched a gruesome scene from a movie. Surround sound. Vivid colors. Curses and chuckles.

"A-Addilyn," Lloyd gasped as Gideon dangled yet another slice of flesh from Lloyd's chest in front of his eyes.

I stared at my rapist, unfeeling…pleased, almost, by his pain and suffering. The fucker deserved it.

"H-have I ever l-lied to you?" Lloyd gasped out, his brow furrowed and his gaze desperate.

"Yes," I heard myself whisper. About Gideon hating me. About giving me the world.

Gideon peeled another stripe off his father's chest, and I didn't grimace. Didn't move as his hoarse screams filled the woodshed.

"Ask him if he killed your mother, princess."

Gideon's voice held no hint of feeling, but the hair on my arms raised from the energy radiating off him, the bloodlust racing through his veins.

My breath came quickly, need of a different sort racing through me. For the first time, I didn't consider our emotions or our desires sick.

I studied Lloyd's knifed-apart body, unmoved by the fear in his eyes. I wanted to snuff it out. "Did you kill her?"

"S-she wasn't right in the head." He swallowed hard, shuddering. "I-I'd f-fallen so in love with you. I ached to be with you, for us to be h-happy together again."

He'd stolen my innocence—and stolen her life.

Heat exploded in my gut. Rage flooded. Consumed like I expected it did Gideon. My body shivered as I soaked that feeling up, but I stepped forward.

"You never made me happy," I hissed, shoulders curling inward, hands clenching at my sides. "You always took without asking. You raped me!" I screamed at him. "A sixteen-year-old girl. You *forced* me!"

"You w-wanted it."

"Give me that knife, Gideon." I held out my hand —steady as fuck—while keeping my focus on Lloyd's face.

Missing a front tooth. Bloody. Haggard. Eyes wide and raging with fear.

The pommel slid along my palm without a word from its owner.

"You thought you could accuse me of disloyalty to him," I whispered at my rapist through clenched teeth, my insides starting to tremble with the need to release my revenge. "The one man who desired to *protect* me. Well."

I grabbed hold of the shriveled length that had made me bleed more times than I could count.

"W-what are you—"

One slice sheared it clear from his body, and Lloyd shrieked as I lifted the dangling flesh in front of his face.

"I'm taking revenge for both of us, you sick fuck." I jammed his dick into his mouth—shoved my fist along behind it, same as he'd done to my young body. "Choke on your own dick, you worthless piece of *shit*."

I rammed the thing down his throat.

Held his jaw in my hand, the knife at my side.

His dark eyes bugged. He tried to cough—

I dropped the knife and clamped his jaw shut tight, my hand grasping at his hair to keep his mouth closed. "Swallow that shit," I hissed at his face, my pulse thrumming. Insides quivering. "Swallow it down like a good little girl," I sneered, not recognizing my own voice.

He thrashed, but Gideon's ropes held him tight. Seconds dragged...and still I stared into his eyes.

Wishing I could bathe in every bit of panic and the haze coming over him.

Stilling.

Twitching.

No more attempts to cough…no more gurgling.

Not a goddamn noise.

Dark eyes dulled beneath a smoothing brow. Face went lax. His head became a dead weight in my hands.

"Princess."

I blinked. Released my hold on Lloyd and jerked back—right into a hard body.

"Addilyn." Gideon wrapped his arms around me gently, tugging me in tight, my back to his chest.

I heaved for oxygen as reality shifted through my brain, finding my consciousness. Shame and regret should have risen, but sweet satisfaction swelled in its place at the gruesome sight of the bloodied corpse in front of me.

"I killed him," I whispered, a hysterical laugh bubbling in my chest. "I made him choke on his own fucking dick!"

"You did." Gideon's voice betrayed his smile, and he nuzzled against my ear, his breath hot.

I shivered, the twinge between my thighs reminding me of how he'd used me earlier. Soreness remained, but I needed him.

"Never seen anything so goddamn sexy, princess." Gideon licked up my neck, and I tilted my head, my gaze still on Lloyd's red and raw slumped body.

"I want you," I told Gideon.

He chuckled and turned me to face him. Dark blue eyes, hooded and full of lust, peered down at me. "I'm hard as fuck and plan to ravage your perfect body, but this shit has to be taken care of first."

I pouted. Actually pouted over the fact that we needed to dispose of a dead body rather than fuck. More reality seeped in, and I glanced at the mess behind me.

Shit.

"How do we hide this, Gideon?" I swallowed hard, a fresh burst of adrenaline weakening my legs. We would be torn apart again. Jailed, no chance of seeing each other…

Shivering, I went willingly against his chest when he pulled me in.

His lips found the top of my head. "I'm going to burn this motherfucking woodshed to the ground until there's nothing left. Bury the ashes and his bones up in the mountains."

"The ground is frozen," I spewed the first thing to come to my mind.

"Not in the old bear cave."

"Huh?"

He kissed me again. "Do you trust me?"

I nodded without hesitation.

"Give me your word, princess. I need to fucking hear it pass your lips."

"Yes," I whispered. Didn't he know I would offer up anything to him? Everything?

He let out a heavy sigh and squeezed me tight, his arms a vise around me. Secure. Protective like no one else in my life had ever been.

"You're safe now," he murmured into my neck. "There's no one left to hurt you, no one to remind you of the shit we're going to leave in the past. We're moving forward, you hear me?"

Stepping back, Gideon held me at arm's length while I fought to keep from shaking. "You and me, got it?"

I couldn't utter a word past the thickness in my throat as the beautiful image of him wavered due to swelling tears. A simple nod seemed enough for him that time around.

"Let's douse this shit with lighter fluid and burn the woodshed down." His grin caused my belly to flutter, but I didn't have the energy to return the outward evidence of how satisfied—happy—I was.

I gripped his hand hard as he led me out into the dark.

34

Gideon

Ten days after ending the fuckface who gave me life, I still dreamed about his screams, the blood. Waking from those good memories always made me happier because of the warm woman pressed against my side. Like she couldn't get close enough.

Every morning, I buried myself in her softness and soaked in her whimpers and moans, her smiles filling me with the sunshine and light my soul had lacked since birth.

My woman. My other half. My goddamn everything.

Deep satisfaction had come from watching Lloyd's body burn and tending the fire then stirring the embers to continue burning. Burying what remained, mere ash, put my past completely behind me.

Me and my princess moved forward. Together.

We packed up all our things, cleaned the cabin, and left Twinkie's place exactly as I'd found it—minus the woodshed, the burned ground covered by a fresh couple of inches of snow.

But if he ever got lucky and managed to escape jail, he would understand.

Without a key, Addilyn was left knocking on her own home's door two hours later. The housekeeper answered, her dark eyes wide and her hair cinched back in a tight knot as usual.

"Miss Addilyn!" She shuffled backward and pulled the door open, her hands twitchy like she wanted to hug my princess.

Addilyn noticed and went to her, showing affection I hadn't ever seen in our months living together in the Reed house by throwing her arms around the Latina woman.

"Everyone thought you were dead," the woman whispered. "And then Mr. Lloyd disappeared as well."

Addilyn stepped back, her eyes wet while glancing around the massive foyer with its marble and garish white everything. Sterile. Lacking in color. But she shone like pure beams of radiant yellow, a shade I used to despise for good reason.

But my princess wore it well.

"Gideon got out of jail, and we took off together," she stated what we'd agreed upon. "Reconnected."

The housekeeper eyed me over Addilyn's shoulder, glancing at the bulk I hadn't carried the last time I'd been beneath that roof.

"It's good to have you back, sir," she said to me, her chin lifting. "The house staff appreciated you looking out for Miss Addilyn all those years ago."

"My pleasure," I grunted.

Her lips twitched, and I remembered Addilyn talking once about the breathing shadows in her mother's employ knowing everything, but they'd signed papers to keep their mouths shut. They had probably taken note of every step I'd taken to rile the princess's feathers. Every word I'd spoken to make her wet, to get her hissing and spitting at me like a cat.

I fucking grinned, sharing a moment with the woman who'd seen more than Addilyn's own mother.

"You said Lloyd isn't here?" Addilyn asked, drawing the housekeeper's gaze off me.

"He went missing ten days ago. No word, no trace."

"Nothing?" Addilyn asked, wrapping her arms around herself.

I stepped forward to tuck her beneath my shoulder, my hand on her hip.

The housekeeper's focus slid to my possessive hold and back up to glance between the two of us standing side by side, a team. "Can I be blunt?"

"Of course," Addilyn answered quietly.

"We saw what he did all those years ago."

Addilyn stiffened against me, but we'd discussed the possibility her abuse hadn't slipped past their eyes from the darkness and beyond.

"Your father wasn't a good man." The housekeeper eyed me without judgement.

I nodded at the woman's statement. She'd get no argument from me.

"Personally—and I can speak for all of those in your employ—I hope he never returns."

Of course they knew.

"*My* employ?" Addilyn asked, her tone wary.

"You're twenty-one. Everything is now yours."

The housekeeper reached out to squeeze Addilyn's arm. "It's good to have you home, Miss Addilyn."

Home.

A huge house neither of us wished to keep—but memories of the staff tugged at my princess's heart. Especially when we'd discussed what to do with the property once Lloyd's ashes rested beneath the ground deep in the cave where we'd buried him.

Without a single tear.

Without a single word of remembrance.

Without a goddamn prayer over his grave.

We'd walked away, hand in hand, one in heart, mind, and spirit.

And we would move forward together in life even though we hadn't spoken of our future.

As far as I was concerned, it was a given. Addilyn Reed was my princess, and no way in fucking hell would we be separated again.

"I'm returning home," Addilyn told the housekeeper, "until I decide what to do with everything."

"I understand."

"And if and when Lloyd shows up, call the cops. That man is no longer welcome in this house."

The housekeeper's lips twitched again. "It would be a pleasure."

"Would either of you care for some lunch?" She glanced between us. "I'm sure I can whip something up—nothing elaborate, but I won't let you go hungry."

"I'd be happy with a can of tomato soup and grilled cheese if you've got it," Addilyn said, her tone revealing a smile.

I looked down to find her face shining with the kind of happiness and peace that wrapped around me like a warm blanket.

"And in the meantime," the housekeeper said, "what would you have us do with Lloyd Destil's things?"

"Box them up and set them out in the garage for when he comes back."

"I owe the man money, so if he never turns up, I won't be the slightest bit upset."

"How much do you owe him?" I asked.

Her chin lifted again. "Too much to ever repay. Hospital bills for my daughter."

"If you decide to stay on as housekeeper for Miss Addilyn and myself, your debt will be erased no matter when that asshole comes looking for money. No questions."

The smile broke over her face. "No questions."

I nodded. According to her tone and the glint in her eyes, our agreement was set in stone.

"Well then." She lightly clapped her hands. "I'll see about getting you both some lunch. Would you like us to ready the master suite for the two of you?"

The woman didn't miss a goddamn thing.

"We'll use Gideon's old room," Addilyn answered what we'd already discussed. "For now."

"I understand."

The woman scattered, leaving the two of us alone to take a trip down memory lane. Addilyn trembled against me, her hand tightening on mine the further into the house's reaches we walked.

There would be no staying, I realized, as every room but my old one had been soiled in her memory forever.

We stood in my bedroom's doorway. It hadn't changed setup wise, but the few things I'd brought from California almost six years earlier had been removed.

Probably tossed in the trash at Lloyd's bidding since I'd been put away with his help.

He'd won that skirmish, but I'd proven the conqueror. I'd ended up with the spoils, the woman we'd both wanted.

"I wish I could burn *this* motherfucker down for you," I murmured, drawing her into my arms, my lips against her hair. "But it's worth more on the market than an insurance claim."

"I have enough money for our kids and grand-kids to live comfortably—and that's if I decide to sell off my father's business."

The whole *I* thing about the money didn't bother me. Our connection, her desire for me, let me know where I stood in terms of our life together. We hadn't discussed it, but we didn't need to. Simply looking into each other's eyes said it all.

"Ever consider California?" I smirked against her hair.

She shrugged and pulled back, smiling up at me. "I'm up for an adventure."

"Then let's move things along and get the fuck out of here. Start over. Clean slate," I stated, lowering my face within inches of hers.

"Okay." My princess brushed her mouth across mine, and same as always when I tasted her on my lips, my dick decided we would need a little more time before taking another step.

The cops showed up exactly like we'd expected.

Just to ask a couple of questions, they'd claimed.

Where was I on the night Jenny had been killed?

At a cabin deep in the woods with Addilyn Reed.

Did I know why my father would park his car out in the middle of nowhere and disappear without a trace?

I had no fucking clue—I'd been at a cabin deep in the woods with Addilyn Reed.

I held my princess's gaze while they continued asking me things, wondering what I'd been up to since getting out of jail. Everything about the calmness on her face and the adoration in her eyes told me the truth before they even asked her to confirm my story.

She would lie for me—I fucking knew it deep in the marrow of my bones. Not one goddamn ounce of fear clenched my gut.

They'd turned to her for the one question that would determine my fate.

"Can you verify his story?"

"Yes." No hesitation, no shame in her eyes. No hint of lying—and I prided myself in reading faces.

Yes.

Best fucking word I'd ever heard from her mouth.

But I kept my grin to myself until the cops left after offering us both a good day.

Then I showed my woman the emotion I struggled to voice, laying waste to her body, claiming every inch, and leaving her limp and sleeping, leaking my cum.

35

Addilyn

One Year Later...

Ciarra threw her arms around me, squeezing me tight against the beaded bodice of her wedding gown. "Thank you for all of this."

My eyes stung with the tears I'd held in throughout the ceremony while standing behind her twin sister, Nissa, and watching as she pledged her life to her long-time boyfriend. "I wish you would have taken advantage of my money even more."

She snorted and stepped back, beaming at me. "Seriously, thank you. What girl has her best friend pay for a wedding like this?"

"One who loves you."

"I couldn't be happier."

I laughed. "Same."

"When's that boy going to put a rock on your hand?"

We both glanced over at Gideon who stood talking with Ciarra's parents who I'd had Midnight Sun Air Charter Services fly into the city a week earlier. He stared at me, his gaze dark and promising, even though he carried on a conversation which doubtless wasn't about getting under my silk dress.

"Don't know, don't care," I answered honestly as warmth rose between my thighs.

"Your love transcends rings and paper."

I smiled, letting the truth shine in how he and I gazed at one another.

"He got revenge for you, and you hid it from me."

I jerked back toward my best friend, my smile fading as my stomach tightened.

"And I understand why," Ciarra murmured with a soft smile, squeezing my hand. "But I love you like my brat of a sister, Nissa, and there's nothing on earth that would ever make me turn on you."

If she knew…

"I *do* know," she stated quietly. "I see it on your face, in your eyes. You took yourself back, took control from him."

My throat tightened as I fought for how to answer—if I even *should* answer.

"I'm glad you did." Ciarra hugged me again when

she realized I wouldn't speak a word to confirm or deny. "He deserves to rot in hell."

I breathed easier, my legs weakened by the shot of adrenaline that had rushed through me over our quiet conversation.

"Where's my wife?" Ciarra's husband strode our way, grinning like a fool happy in love. He winked at me over his shoulder while drawing her away toward others wanting to congratulate the newlyweds.

Both he and his parents had thanked me profusely for paying for the entire affair as my gift to my best friend.

The dresses, the hall, the catering, the flowers, the DJ...I refused to let Ciarra dish out money for a single thing.

Her parents still lived off-grid with little to their name, and I wouldn't allow my best friend to have anything but the wedding of her dreams.

I'd wired the money to her from our home in the Cayman Islands where we'd moved three months after selling my parents' house and my father's business.

We had enough money to live comfortably for three lifetimes.

I felt Gideon's energy before his arm slipped around my waist, and I melted against his hard body, soaking up his warmth, his security.

A latecomer slipped through the hall's doors as

we stood in silence, the sight of him causing us both to stiffen.

Leo.

We watched silently as he moved through the room, greeting Ciarra and her new husband.

The information Gideon had sent to the FBI had cleared Leo's uncle and landed Devon's father behind bars—where his life ended in a dark corner. Stab wounds had littered his body.

Rogers had already been released from the jail by that time which meant someone else had taken out that bit of trash.

Gideon felt sure his friend Twinkie had gotten revenge for his lover but hadn't ever gone to visit as agreed upon by both men.

We hadn't spoken with Leo since that day in the diner. No one had made the connection between Roger's release, Devon's conviction for killing Jenny, or Lloyd's disappearance.

And if they had suspicions, nothing and no one emerged to point at either of us.

Lloyd obviously hadn't ever returned.

Devon sat behind bars regardless of his claims of innocence, all the evidence gathered from the motel room pointing to one suspect.

Gideon had initially feared Devon would remember a third party being with the two of them that night. His lips thinned and brow furrowed every time we'd discussed the possibility Devon had heard Jenny say his name.

But Devon had claimed complete ignorance of what transpired that night.

He'd fallen asleep on his couch—same as I'd done when drugged by Gideon—and woke the next morning atop Jenny's corpse.

"I almost killed him that night."

I jerked my focus off Leo toward Gideon. "What? Who?"

"Leo." Gideon continued to stare at Leo while I studied his face, my brain trying to process what he'd meant.

"What are you talking about?"

"That night you went out for pizza with him."

My date…the baby steps…

I'd felt Gideon's energy while on my date with Leo, but I'd reasoned it away as wishful thinking.

"You were there, weren't you?"

"Yes." Still, he peered at the old friend I hadn't kept in touch with even though Ciarra had.

"What do you mean you almost killed him?"

"I watched him walk you to your car, and I followed, sticking to the shadows. He flirted and touched you. The fucker's lucky I didn't slice his neck open like I was tempted to do when he strode past me toward his own car."

So that explained Gideon's strange behavior the day we'd met Leo at the diner.

"*You're* lucky—and Rogers is lucky you didn't slice his neck."

"True." Gideon glanced down at him, his focus slipping to my lips I'd coated with shimmering gloss. "Let's get out of here, princess."

His eyes promised he'd ease the ache between my thighs I'd been dealing with upon seeing him all cleaned up in a suit, something I hadn't gotten to enjoy since our parents' wedding day.

Three hours later, I lay exhausted on the hotel's bed, my body sore, achy, and completely sated.

"You're a beast," I muttered with a smile, no heat in my voice.

"And you're my beauty, princess."

I snorted. "There's nothing fairy tale about our story, Gideon Destil."

"We're just a couple of kinky, sick fucks—"

"We're not sick," I reminded him, having completely come to grips with who and what we were—perfect together.

Two souls desperate for each other, unable to slake our thirst. We might have been forbidden at one point in our lives, but our obsessions hadn't faded or lessened in the slightest.

"I won't apologize for wanting you, princess," Gideon spoke as though reading my mind. "Won't ever apologize for taking you either."

"Good."

"That's all you've got to say?"

I shrugged and curled against his side, soaking in his heat, uncaring of the damp sweat still clinging to his skin. "I could add that I love you."

"I love you too—and to me, that means you're mine." He squeezed me tight, and I closed my eyes, resting in his arms.

"I always was."

THE END

About the Author

Lynn Burke is an international bestselling and award-winning author. A stay-at-home mom, she's a lover of coffee and vino, and with three spawn and two fur babies underfoot, noise levels dictate the daily switch-over time. In her few quiet 'me' moments, she can be found hunched over her Mac, trying to type as fast as her muse spews hot stories.

You can find more about Lynn at her website: www.authorlynnburke.com

Also By Lynn Burke

Abel's Obsession

Divulging Secrets

Healing Storms

In Between

Reluctant Lumberjack

Resisting his Mate

The Playboy Bachelor

Billion Dollar Love Anthology

Blood Born Series

Bonds of Worship Series

Dark Leopards MC

Darkest Desires Series

Devil's Outlaws MC

Elite Escort Series

Fallen Gliders MC

Forbidden Obsession Duet

Found by Fate Series

Midnight Sun Series

Missing Link Series

Risso Family Series

Sandy Ridge Series

Vicious Vipers MC

www.ingramcontent.com/pod-product-compliance
Lightning Source LLC
Chambersburg PA
CBHW071234190726
48292CB00007B/2276